# No More Regrets

www.tamra.lassiter.com

# No More Regrets

### Tamra Lassiter

To Mary,
Thanks for all
you do!
Love,　:)
　Tammy

This is a work of fiction. Certain real locations are mentioned, however all names, characters, events and incidents described in this book are fictitious or a product of the author's imagination. Any resemblance to real persons, living or deceased, is entirely coincidental.

NO MORE REGRETS

ISBN-13: 978-1-942235-91-0 (trade paperback)
ISBN-13: 978-1-942235-90-3 (e-book)

www.tamralassiter.com

For the Lassiters

# *Chapter One*

## *Jackson*

She would be noticed in any crowd. But, in this one made up of families on vacation and a senior tour group from Idaho, she can't be missed. More than one guy looks her way—a few jealous women, too. She has wavy brown hair that cascades down her back and a body with curves in all the right places.

My SEAL training taught me to notice things that other people might miss, but anyone paying the least bit of attention would pick up on her nervousness. She doesn't look at anyone as she walks down the street. She keeps her gaze focused straight ahead, which only increases her mystery. That in itself isn't a big deal, but her hands are shaking as she fidgets with the strap on her shoulder bag as she hurriedly walks past me. Her eyes may be focused on the path in front of her, but they're widened, too. She has *woman in distress* written all over her.

*Money.* That's the other thing written all over her. She has *lots* of it. Expensive, well-tailored clothes. Large diamond earrings. High-end purse. Yep, money. And *way* out of my league on multiple levels.

Smitty clears his throat and gives me a knowing look.

"Nice, huh?"

"I guess she is, if you're into women with too much attitude and too much money."

*And apparently, I am. I can't take my eyes off of her.*

"The *too much money* would sure be nice," Smitty says with a smile. "Gotta run, man. Gotta get home and spend some time with the wife before I get to work. She's not rich and she doesn't have attitude— most of the time anyway—but best of all, she's mine."

The corners of Smitty's mouth tip up to form a smile, but the sincerity doesn't reach his eyes. Is he feeling guilty for ogling a woman that isn't his wife?

"And I gotta get on the road. Good seeing you, Smitty."

We exchange a few pats on the back and head out. Smitty turns toward the alley that leads to the parking lot behind the restaurant. I should turn left, the direction of my truck, but instead, I walk in the opposite direction, toward the mystery woman. *I feel pulled toward her.* It sure doesn't hurt that she has a nice ass.

## Chapter Two

### Emmy

It's barely summer on the calendar, but the season has been with us for a good few weeks. Days turn from cool to warm, and the humidity slips into the day little by little and then the night. Then suddenly summer is upon us, and there will be little relief from the heat until the fall.

The sun beats down hard now as I walk to my *meeting*. The sky is cloudless, showing only a beautiful blue. A bead of sweat trickles down my back, pooling there with other drops that came before it. I'm so glad that I shed my jacket before coming out into this overpowering heat. The tiniest breeze wisps through the air. I take a deep breath to keep the cool feeling with me.

The campus is quiet this time of year, but the throng of tourists on D.O.G. Street makes up for it in droves. They have no idea that's what we call the famous Duke of Gloucester Street that cuts through the heart of Historic Williamsburg. They would most likely wince at the crudity. The thought lifts the corners of my mouth into a small smile. The duke himself probably wouldn't be too thrilled about the nickname either.

I pick up my pace as I make a right onto Nassau Street. *Why did I have to work those extra twenty minutes?* It couldn't be helped, but now I'm late. Late for my meeting and probably late to pick up the kids. *I can still make it.* I'm always in a rush, and since I make it most of the time, I have little incentive to change my ways.

I turn the corner onto the lawn of the old First Baptist Church and let out a huge sigh. He's still here, thank goodness, waiting for me beneath the shade of a large oak tree. A look of relief washes over his face. Maybe he was worried I might stand him up.

He has dark skin, dark, short hair, and dark, almost black eyes. He looks Latino, and he's dressed in khaki shorts and a t-shirt advertising a bait shop. Much different than the older man with graying hair that I pictured. That's what I get for allowing myself to get an impression from an email. It's not like I care. As long as he brought the money, I'm golden.

"Are you Mr. Lehman?"

He nods. "And you're Ms. Bennett. So nice to meet you." He extends his hand to me, and we shake lightly. "Can I see it?"

I open my handbag and take out the velvet box, turning it toward him so that he can see the diamond and sapphire tennis bracelet inside. He gives me a big smile as he extends his index finger to rub along the stones.

"Beautiful."

"Do you have my money?" My voice hitches slightly. Hopefully, Mr. Lehman didn't notice. I want to appear confident and comfortable with this transaction, but back-alley bartering isn't something I'm used to.

"Five thousand dollars. I have it right here." He reaches into the pocket of his cargo shorts, fumbles briefly.

Not his wallet.

*A gun.*

My breath is taken away as the shock floods my system. I know nothing about guns, but it's there in his hand, and it's pointed right at me.

My eyes are drawn to it. The dark metal radiates cold, even in this heat. Another light breeze wafts through the air, this one bringing out goose bumps on my exposed skin. *Stay strong.* Battle the panic. I can't allow myself the indulgence of falling apart.

Another man walks out from behind the wide trunk of the tree. He also has a gun. *What the hell?*

They speak to each other in Spanish and then laugh heartily

"Hand over the bracelet, along with your purse."

*Thank you God that my children aren't with me.* Not that I would ever bring them on an errand like this, but I'm thankful that they're safe. Still, they need me to be alive to take care of them, and I need the money from selling the bracelet. I can't just turn it over to them.

Options. Do I have any? The mass of tourists are just down the block. I chose this spot—an open lawn that's slightly off the beaten path and blocked by a line of trees—because I wanted some privacy for this transaction. *Way to go, Emmy.* It seemed like a good idea at the time.

If I could get back to D.O.G. then I would be safe. Odds aren't good that I would make it, though. I'm obviously outnumbered. Plus, I'm sure they run faster than I do, so if they didn't shoot me first, they could easily overpower me and take what they want. Since I have no firearms with me, I try the only thing I do have—my big mouth.

"Look. Why don't we just stop all this before it gets out of hand? It's obvious to me that you forgot your wallet. I haven't gotten a good look at you, so I won't have anything to say to anyone about what happened here today. Let's just go our separate ways."

Mr. Lehman's eyes are hard. He takes a step toward me.

"Hand them..." He doesn't finish his sentence as he's tackled from behind in a blur of movement. His gun falls from his hand, and with what seems like little effort on the part of my savior, Mr. Lehman falls to the ground in a crumpled heap. The other guy seems just as surprised as I am. He turns to his partner, but his nanosecond of inaction is all the time needed for him to be overpowered as well. His gun is deftly kicked from his hand. That move is followed by a punch, and he's down for the count.

My hero stops and walks toward me. He's not wearing a cape or a mask, he's just a normal guy wearing a golf shirt and jeans—jeans that hug his muscular legs and butt like they were made only for him. *Don't think about his butt.* He's huge, well over six feet tall and built, like really built. His chest is hard against his shirt, his tanned forearms bulge from the sleeves. His buzzed haircut, along with the emblem on his shirt, makes it easy to deduce that he's a Navy man. He isn't young though, probably a little older than I am, late thirties, maybe or early forties.

The relief that it's over finally registers. My breath leaves my body in a whoosh. My knees weaken. I move my feet to try to support myself. Blackness invades my vision. I fight in vain to keep it at bay, but it quickly takes over until there's no light, only darkness.

## Chapter Three

### Jackson

She's down for the count—not a surprise after all this.

She falls into my arms, so light and helpless, and I slowly lower her to the grass. Kneeling next to her, I check her pulse. Her skin is soft and warm. She'll come around in a few minutes. The other two will be out longer.

I retrieve my phone from my pocket and dial 9-1-1. The operator is brisk and efficient with many questions. I keep my answers as short as possible and disconnect. There will be a lot more explaining to do when the police arrive. This little incident better not screw up my leaving town. How could I not get involved? Whatever this is, I had to help her. There was no question about that.

Thank God I followed her. So why is someone who appears to be so loaded trying to sell a bracelet to a couple of hoodlums?

*Flowers.*

She smells like flowers. I breathe in her warm scent. Why not? She isn't married—no ring on her finger—so I'm going with the theory that she isn't taken. *Sure hope that's true.* I don't need to be ogling someone else's woman. It's not like there's going to be a future for the two of us, but I have to admit that I'm attracted to her. She's a hottie, even though she's a bit on the short side. What's the nice word for that? Petite? She's petite. There's something vibrant about her spirit that I'm attracted to even more— what Mom would call an *old soul.*

Geez. The way she tried to argue her way out of a gunfight. The girl's got spunk. The corners of my mouth pull up to form a smile. And then there was the slightest hint of southern drawl when she spoke. *I love it.*

She's still out. I brush her cheek lightly with the back of my hand—creamy pale skin and perfect pink lips with just a touch of pink lipgloss remaining. She stirs. Her golden brown eyes open. They're dazed at first, but I watch as the cloudiness clears.

## Chapter Four

*Emmy*

The man leans over me, the one who saved me. His eyes are the most beautiful blue I've ever seen, like the aqua ocean in Grand Cayman where we used to rent a house for spring break. He smiles, revealing tiny crinkles of lines at the corners of his eyes. His face is the healthy tan color of someone who spends time outdoors but not too much time. The branches of the oak tree behind him complete the backdrop of a beautiful picture.

"Good. You're coming around. Don't worry. You're going to be fine." His voice, deep and manly, somehow reverberates in my chest, even though he's speaking softly.

*What is he saying? Me fine? How can I ever be fine?*

"What happened?" I lean up on my elbows.

"You fainted." I did? "You were only out for a minute. Don't get up yet, though. I've called 9-1-1. Help will be here soon."

No argument here. My arms and legs have a Jello-like quality about them right now.

Oh yeah. My meeting with Mr. Lehman.

*He had a gun.*

I'm lying on the grass in the same spot where I fell. I didn't just fall though. I remember the feeling of his arms around me as the blackness closed in. But what happened after that? I don't like thinking about being touched by a man—a stranger no less—and not remembering what happened.

"Would you like some water?"

He holds up a water bottle and gestures to me. His hands. They're huge.

*Do not think about how those hands were on my body just a few moments ago.*

A fresh round of dizziness takes me, and my head sways slightly. His eyes widen with concern.

"Here, please drink some."

He holds the bottle closer. It's only half full. His lips have been on that bottle. I push the thought out of my head before I actually faint again.

"No, thank you." I ease up a little more and register the sight of my two attackers lying on the grass a few feet away. *Please God, let them be unconscious and not dead.* "Are they going to be okay?"

He nods. "They'll be fine. The EMTs will be here soon, and they can check you out, too."

"No. I don't want an ambulance. I don't have time for all that. As a matter of fact, I have to go." I move to get up, but the dizziness quickly returns. *Crud.* I settle back down to a sitting position, so he doesn't know that I'm still feeling as woozy as I am.

"You can't get up yet. You need to see a doctor."

Sirens can be heard now. The ambulance is getting close. *What a mess.* There's no time for this.

"Plus, you'll have to give the police a statement."

The tears begin to well up in my eyes. *Be strong and tough.* That attitude has gotten me through so much. But, I was just held at gunpoint for goodness sake. A little crying is expected, right? His face is full of concern as he sits down next to me on the grass. He hands me the bottle of water, and this time I take a sip. The cold liquid stings my throat. I hand the empty bottle back to him and wipe the tears from my cheeks with the back of my hand. The relief starts a whole new round of tears. There's no controlling them now.

"Thank you."

He puts a hand on my shoulder and squeezes lightly.

"I'm glad that I was here."

"My name is Emmy." I hold out my hand.

"I'm Jackson." He shakes my hand gently. My

hand feels so small in his—probably because it is. His handshake lingers, my brown eyes meeting his, bright blue. It would be easy to get lost in those eyes. Some woman is very lucky to get to look into them every night. Someone like him *has* to be taken.

"That's a nice name," I finally choke out and remove my hand from his grasp.

"Technically, that's my last name, but that's what everyone calls me."

"What you did was pretty amazing. Are you always such a badass?" He shrugs as if his actions were nothing out of the ordinary.

"When I need to be. So what exactly were you doing with these two?" He gestures towards my attackers.

I'm saved from answering by the arrival of the police. The siren is so loud at first, but fortunately it's turned off as soon as they arrive. They cut the lights as well. The less publicity about this event, the better. *Please don't let me be seen by anyone that I know*. Two officers exit their patrol car and walk in our direction. Jackson stands and walks towards them.

## Chapter Five

## *Jackson*

*Here we go.*

The policemen exit their vehicle quickly, their eyes moving over the scene. I walk toward them with my hands out to my sides. It's not a hands-up kind of motion and definitely non-threatening. I have nothing to hide and did nothing wrong. They just have to come to that conclusion on their own.

The first policeman to reach me is a few inches shorter than I am, around six feet tall. He has reddish-blond hair, cut military-neat. He's fairly young, probably in his mid-twenties and pretty fit. His green eyes study me. The other policeman is much older, fifty at least, his short brown hair peppered with gray. He's not what I'd call *fit*, but he hasn't completely let himself go either.

They both stop about three feet away from me. The redhead has his hand placed near his gun.

"I'm unarmed." *Good to get that out of the way in the beginning.* "I'm going to put my hand in my right pocket and get my wallet."

The older guy nods. I retrieve my wallet slowly and carefully as promised, take out my driver's license, and hand it to him. The redhead kneels next to the closest criminal and checks his pulse. A large sigh escapes. No homicides today, at least not here. He moves to the other guy.

"My name is Ed Jackson. I came upon these two men holding this woman at gunpoint. I disarmed them and called you."

The policemen both look at Emmy. She's sitting in the same spot under the tree. Her eyes are still a bit dazed, but her color is coming back. Good sign.

"I'm Officer Murphy," the older man says. He holds out his hand and shakes mine. I feel relief knowing that although this isn't over, they no longer consider me an immediate threat. "This is Officer Alden." The young man nods from where he kneels next to one of the criminals. He rolls him over and cuffs his hands behind him. "We need to ask you both some questions about what happened here."

"Of course."

We both move towards Emmy. Officer Murphy kneels down next to her and introduces himself. It's good she doesn't try to stand up because although she's trying to exude the vibe that all is fine, she's definitely *not* fine. I kneel down as well.

The wailing ambulance arrives. A handful of curious onlookers have gathered. Nothing draws a crowd like the possibility of gore and death. They peer around the corner of the tree line to get a look at what all the commotion's about. Emmy's complexion now has a hint of green. She's obviously uncomfortable with all this attention.

The paramedics exit their vehicle. There's a man and a woman. The man is African-American. He's very young, could be a college student, and his head is shaved bald. The woman paramedic is also young, with long, dark hair that she's pulled back into a ponytail. Both of them carry boxes of gear. After a nod from the officers, each bends down next to a man lying on the grass. They lift each wrist to check their pulses. My attention shifts back to Emmy.

## Chapter Six

### Emmy

Officer Alden walks to our little group and kneels down as well. I feel kind of bad to make the three men sit down at my level, but it's good that they are. I'm not well enough to stand yet. There are no benches around and nowhere else to sit. So, I don't mention it, and they don't either.

Another car arrives—this one has no identifying marks. However it's clearly a police car. A man and a woman exit. The police officers stand and walk to the newcomers. The woman's dressed in a stylish black pantsuit with low heels. Does she have to apprehend criminals in those shoes? She's young— late twenties, I'd guess. Her dark hair is straight, almost as jet black as her outfit. She wears it cut short in a style reminiscent of a flapper. Her hairstyle is the only thing that seems fun about her. The rest of her is all business, especially her dark, piercing eyes. Her eyes take in the scene and finally settle on mine.

"I'm Detective Patterson, and this is Detective Marshall."

Detective Marshall is almost the opposite of Patterson, if there could be such a thing. He's male and older, pushing sixty at least. Everything about him is softer, from his blond hair to his light blue eyes to his round belly. He takes my hand and shakes it softly.

"Is it okay if we begin the questioning? Are you up for it now?"

His eyes are focused on me, and they show his concern. Detective Patterson is watching me as well, but her gaze feels more invasive.

"Sure. My name is Emmy by the way, Emilou Bennett." I shake each of their hands. "I'm already late to pick up my kids. Would it be okay if I text my friend to ask her to take them to swim practice?"

Detective Marshall gives me a nod, and I quickly text Anne. I wish I didn't have to ask her to help me... again. She'll understand after I explain, but why do I feel like I'm always explaining something? I depend on her way too much.

"Miss Bennett, excuse me, is it Mrs. or Miss?" Detective Patterson retrieves a notebook and pen from her bag and begins taking notes.

"Miss. I'm not married." The heat of my blush begins creeping up my cheeks. Why should I be embarrassed to be a *Miss?* I have no clue, but, after everything that's happened, that's what I'm feeling.

"Miss Bennett," Detective Patterson's tone is firm. It's not mean, just not exactly nice. She really needs to work on her people skills. "Please start from the beginning, and tell us what happened."

A long sigh escapes.

"I have a bracelet that I was trying to sell on Craig's List."

*The bracelet!*

As if reading my mind, Jackson reaches next to my bag and hands me the black velvet box. I pinch it open to see the bracelet shining back at me, intact, looking just as it did only moments ago when I arrived. Relief spills over me from my head to my toes, causing another sigh. The last thing that I need to do is lose this.

"I'm sorry." A couple deep breaths help me to gather myself to begin again. "The man on the right there, Mr. Lehman, or at least that's what he said his name was, agreed to pay me five thousand dollars for the bracelet. I met him here to make the exchange."

"Is the bracelet stolen?"

"No." A frustrated sigh escapes. "It was an anniversary gift."

"Okay. The bracelet is obviously worth more than

five thousand dollars. Why would you sell it for so little?"

All eyes are on me now, the heat of their gazes making me want to squirm. I look up and find Jackson's first. I take another deep breath to steel myself and continue carefully. I don't want the whole world knowing my business, which is why I came here in the first place.

"The bracelet is worth twelve thousand dollars. The appraisal is in my purse. I was trying to sell it on Craig's List because the pawnshop I took it to said they wouldn't buy it, and I need the money. I didn't do anything wrong or break any laws. It's mine to sell." My voice is a little squeaky by the end of my speech, but I'm hoping that they didn't notice.

Detective Patterson's eyes narrow with obvious disapproval. Now that is just unnecessary. *Hello! I'm the victim here.* Maybe that's why Detective Marshall takes over the questioning.

"Why don't you tell us what happened when you arrived to meet Mr. Lehman?"

I tell them my story and explain how Jackson came out of nowhere, kicked butt, and took names. Jackson sits quietly during my explanation, but our eyes meet again as I tell the tale. His eyes are soft and understanding and concerned. They are definitely not what I would expect from a man who took down two armed men like it was the easiest thing he'd ever done.

Mr. Lehman moves suddenly and tries to sit up.

He cries out in Spanish. Officer Alden helps him stand. He looks directly at Jackson and snarls something at him. Jackson answers, also in Spanish. I have no idea what he just said, but the words roll off his tongue effortlessly. Officer Alden pulls Mr. Lehman over to the patrol car and gets him settled in the backseat.

My phone chirps with a return text from Anne.

*Got the kids. No problem.*

Thank goodness. Anne and I have the good fortune of being friends and having children the same age who get along. Truthfully, I don't know what I'd do without her. She's one of the few people in the neighborhood who doesn't judge me.

"What did he say?" I finally ask Jackson. My curiosity is killing me.

"He told me to go...um do something to myself. Let's just leave it at that."

"And what did you say back to him?"

"I told him he's going to get a lot of that kind of action in jail."

I smile, and Jackson returns it with a chuckle. His eyes lighten, and then his whole face comes alive. Why on earth am I thinking about his eyes and his smile? I know nothing about this man other than that he can kick some major butt.

Officer Alden returns, and Detective Marshall begins the questioning again. "Mr. Jackson, why don't you tell us how you came to join the party?"

*Good question.*

"I'm here touring Colonial Williamsburg for the day. I had just had lunch with an old Navy friend and was standing outside the restaurant when Emmy walked by. She was in a hurry and looking extremely anxious, so I was curious. I've been a SEAL for most of my twenty years in the Navy, so I know a lot about human behavior."

Navy SEAL. Yep, that explains his ability to kick ass. Jackson turns his eyes from Detective Marshall's, and they lock with mine as he continues.

"I wanted to see what she was up to, so I followed her. I almost stopped twice because I felt so ridiculous. I'm supposed to be retired and on vacation, but I just couldn't help it. Old habits die hard, I guess. I had to see what was going down, so I kept following her. I could tell from the beginning that this wasn't going down as she'd planned. It just had a bad vibe. Then I caught sight of the man hiding behind the tree, and I knew for sure that he was trouble. I moved around to get a better vantage point, but before I could get there, the other guy stepped out from behind the tree and trained another gun on Emmy. So, I jumped them both and separated the assailants from their weapons."

He makes it sound so simple, but I'm sure it wasn't.

"Once they were incapacitated, I moved to see how Emmy was holding up. That's when she fainted. I caught her and laid her down on the grass. She was out for approximately two minutes. I called 9-1-1 right away. What a mess this was. Three people on the ground, and I was the only one standing. If someone had walked by at that moment, there's no telling what they would have thought."

Jackson chuckles, and the policemen join in. How is any of this funny? Clearly I am missing the joke.

Mr. Lehman's partner wakes up with a shout while the paramedics are working on him. They move away to allow Officer Alden to escort him to the waiting patrol car. He and Mr. Lehman both scowl at us from the backseat. The female paramedic walks over to our little group and asks permission to examine me. It's not like I really have a choice. At least the exam is quick and painless. She asks me to stand and walk a little. It takes some concentration, but I think I look steady on my feet, even if I am faking it. It feels more like I've been drinking, and I'm trying to pass the sobriety test. Not that I would know what that feels like, but I have an imagination. The detectives and Jackson continue their conversation, but even so, I feel Jackson's gaze on me the entire time.

They release me after I promise to follow up with my primary care doctor. I take my seat under the tree. The officers continue their questioning, which consists of Jackson and me repeating our stories a few more times. The officers finally announce that we're done for now.

"Mr. Jackson," Detective Marshall begins, "I hate to say this, but you'll have to hang around town for a day or so while we get our reports written up. We will get on it as soon as we can, but it may be tomorrow before we're able to release you to continue on your trip."

Jackson doesn't look upset by the news. "That's pretty much what I expected. No worries here."

*Well, I'm worried.* I don't want to delay Jackson.

"And, it's possible that you might have to come back to town if this ever goes to trial."

*Ugh. But if he hadn't been here to save me...*

Jackson smiles and shakes Detective Marshall's hand.

"Understood."

The detectives give us both their business cards, and we give them our addresses and phone numbers. Mr. Lehman and his partner are driven away in the police cruiser, their stares boring holes in us as they go.

I'm left alone with Jackson, feeling completely awkward. I'm not used to being the damsel in distress. What do I say? My eyes meet his, and I decide to say the only thing that I can think of.

"Thank you again."

The words are heartfelt, but they feel insufficient, even as they leave my mouth. Three small words. Not nearly enough for what he did for me. The wetness returns to my eyes as the enormity of the situation takes hold.

*There was a gun pointed at me. No, there were two guns pointed at me.*

*I could have died.*

Jackson squeezes my arm gently.

"You don't have to thank me."

A tear escapes and drops down the slope of my cheek. He moves his hand—I think to wipe it—but if that's what he planned to do, he changes his mind. His hand comes to rest at his side.

"I'd be happy to drive you somewhere if you'd like. You may have fooled the others, but I know you aren't as steady as you're letting on."

"I'm fine, really." *Sound confident. You can break down later.* "I wouldn't be though if you hadn't come along when you did."

I force a smile, but it feels weak. I'm not fooling him.

"At least let me walk you to your car. Where are you parked?"

"This way."

That can't hurt. We start walking around the line of trees and back to D.O.G. Street.

## Chapter Seven

### Jackson

I keep a close eye on Emmy as we walk, and I stay as close to her as I can without freaking her out. If she goes down again, I need to be ready to catch her. The color has returned to her cheeks, but she's definitely still shaky. And having an excuse to watch her makes me feel like less of a stalker. Because, let's face it, I can't keep my eyes off of her. Her wavy chestnut hair falls down her back. She turns her head slightly to look at me and brushes a piece of hair away from her face.

"Are you here visiting with your family?"

Is this her way of asking if I'm single? *Don't read anything into it, you moron.* It's just a question. She has kids. She's probably just making conversation. It's not like it matters.

"No. Just me, doing a little sight-seeing."

"You said you are here visiting for the day. Where are you from?" *Yeah, she's definitely just making conversation.*

"I was stationed in Little Creek, near Virginia Beach. I'm on my way to San Diego—just left this morning. This is my first stop on the way."

"You're driving all the way to San Diego?" Her surprise is evident in her tone.

"Yeah. I'm moving there. I just retired from the Navy, and I'm going out there to open a security firm with my buddy, Marco."

"If you need a reference, I can attest that you'd make a great body guard."

The corners of her lips tip upward to form a small smile. It's like a lightning bolt straight to my groin. *Knock it off.* I'm forced to clear the lump from my throat before I can continue.

"It's not that kind of security, actually. Believe it or not, nothing physical—only computers. Our firm will deal with cyber-security. We're hoping to get some work with the government and some local businesses."

"Well, if you ever need a back-up plan, you're all set." She smiles again. My gaze is fixated on that smile and her perfect, pink lips. What would they feel like? What would they taste like?

*Snap out of it.* That isn't going to happen.

"I'm parked right over here." I point towards the small parking lot. "I can give you a ride to your car if it's much farther."

*Because the less walking she does, the better.*

She studies her watch. It's a Cartier, another pricey piece of jewelry. Maybe she's weighing whether or not it's a good idea to accept a ride from an almost-stranger.

"My van is in one of the William and Mary lots, and it would be nice to have a ride. Thanks."

My Ford pickup has an extended cab, but the back seat is stuffed full of duffel bags and a few boxes and other things that I didn't put in the moving truck. I wasn't expecting company, but luckily I've barely started on my journey, so the only junk I've accumulated on the front bench seat is a newspaper and a paper coffee cup.

Emmy climbs up and into the cab like it's second nature. Women I've dated in the past complained or at least sighed heavily as they negotiated the running boards, clumsily grabbed onto the handle, and heaved themselves inside. A wealthy woman should be extremely put out.

Emmy buckles up and begins giving me directions. I take a right turn and head towards her van. Van huh? She seems like more of a Mercedes kind of woman. She's full of surprises. She continues her questioning.

"Where else will you be stopping on your journey?"

"Probably Nashville, but I've set aside a month for my trip so that I can stop anywhere I'd like to on the way to California. I plan to spend some time with my parents in Albuquerque. There are lots of places in the U.S. that I'd like to see that I haven't—like Williamsburg, for example. I lived practically down the street for years, but never really had the time to come here to see it. So I guess you're a local?"

Our time together is almost up. I *have* to know more about her.

"Yeah. My family's from Arkansas. I grew up there, but I've lived in Williamsburg since I came to college here at William and Mary. That was seventeen years ago. I got married and stayed."

"What happened to your husband? Divorced?"

*Who am I kidding? I have to know the answer to this one.*

"Yeah."

She's still a little pale from her ordeal, but I don't think it's my imagination that the pallor of her skin slides even a shade lighter at the mention of her divorce. No time for further questioning though, because we're here. I pull into the empty space beside her minivan.

"Thank you... again, and thanks for the ride."

She opens the door to get out. It seems strange to just let her leave, but what am I supposed to do? My hand moves to her arm.

"Wait. Are you sure you're okay? I'm worried about you driving."

She turns towards me and flashes me a smile that doesn't reach her eyes.

"I'm fine." *She's not fine.* "Really. Good luck on your trip. Maybe I'll see you again if we have to go to court or whatever. I'm sorry, though, if you have to come back from California."

"Don't worry about that. Please be careful." *Please.*

She nods her head in response and climbs down out of my truck as fluidly as she got in. She gives me a little wave, tips her head, and that's the end of my time with Miss Emilou Bennett.

## Chapter Eight

### Emmy

Catching my breath is harder than it should be. I'm finally alone for the first time since this whole *ordeal* began, and I need to breathe. It's an almost impossible task in the heat of this car, but it doesn't matter. I don't have that luxury right now anyway.

I need to get out of here.

I need to get to my kids.

That's not the only reason that I need to keep it together. Jackson's eyes are still on me. His truck is still parked in the spot next to mine. He doesn't believe my declarations that all is well. That doesn't really matter though. I'm happy for what Jackson did for me—I can't even think about what might have happened if he hadn't followed me—but he has his life, and I have mine.

I sneak a look in Jackson's direction and flash him the best smile that I can muster right now. *Think "hope to see you again" and not "hysterical woman on the edge."*

*Time to go.* I pull the gearshift down into reverse and slide back out of my parking space. I increase the wattage of my smile—hopefully—and give him a quick wave. The smile even feels a little genuine in celebration of the fact that I just successfully backed out of my parking space. Sometimes it's the little things. I may be a mental disaster right now, but I can do this. I will power through it like I do with everything else. Just get through the things I have to do today. Then I can open a bottle of wine and have a mommy meltdown all on my own, when no one will ever know, especially a handsome stranger that I just met and will never see again.

I shift into drive and ease forward, slowly navigating the parking lot, and then maneuver the car onto the road in the direction of home. My lips curl up into a smile again. This time it's genuine and just for me. *I can so do this.*

Visions of the gun barrel flash in my mind.

But I was saved.

*Just hold on a little longer.*

The horror of it hits me again. I push it away and focus on the traffic ahead of me. The images creep back and with them come the tears.

What are a few tears? I can cry a little while I'm driving. I'm a pro at multi-tasking. No one will see me. When I get to the kids I can make an excuse for my puffy eyes. *Good plan.*

Resistance is futile anyway, so I surrender to the tears and let them come. Once released, they come in full force. The relief is immense. Thinking of what could have been. It's almost too much to handle. My hands tremble, and my body follows. Quivering uncontrollably now, I jerk the car into the parking lot of the nearest strip mall and pull into the first space I come to. I shove the gear shift into park and let it overtake me—the trembling, the tears, all mixed into one huge expression of relief and fear of what could have been.

A squeal escapes when my door opens. A blurry Jackson stands close to me—at least that's how he looks through the veil of tears. How should I feel about seeing him? I don't even know. Relief comes first. This is the second time today that he's come to me in my time of need. Embarrassment quickly follows though, as this is not how I want to be seen in front of anyone, especially someone who's as good looking as Jackson. Of course, he followed me here, and that kind of pisses me off.

All these feelings course through me and collide in the pit of my stomach.

"Why did you follow me?"

His concerned eyes show trepidation. *A hysterical woman requires caution, I suppose.*

"I just wanted to make sure you got home okay. I knew that you weren't okay to drive. This one's my fault. I never should have let you get behind the wheel." He speaks slowly and calmly as he studies me some more. "Can I please drive you home or wherever you need to go? I can't let you drive and keep a clear conscience, especially after the spectacle I just witnessed."

*Spectacle? Now that really pisses me off.*

Why is Jackson telling me what's good for me? He doesn't know me, and he's definitely not the boss of me anyway. *Geez. Very mature.* I sound like Audrey. She threw those same words at me just this morning. Still, he's ticking me off, especially because I know he's right.

*Great.* I could have killed myself twice today. I don't answer him verbally, but I grab my purse and my school bag off the passenger seat. Jackson steps back and holds the door open for me. Then he turns and opens the passenger door of his truck. I climb inside for the second time today. The flow of tears is finally beginning to ebb, and I'm left with lots of post-cry snot. *Just lovely.* I reach for one of the napkins stacked on his console and blow. *Not attractive.* But, it's not like I have a choice at this point. The nose blowing is better than the alternative. Jackson starts his truck and sits quietly behind the wheel, looking straight out the front window.

## *Chapter Nine*

### *Jackson*

I learned ages ago that sometimes it's best to just let women cry it out. Emmy's current situation wasn't my doing, so I let her go. That said, it's hard to listen to a woman cry. Every tear and sniffle just makes me more and more angry. Angry at the men who tried to rob her and angry at Emmy, herself. I mean, what the hell was she thinking trying to sell something like a diamond bracelet to strangers in a deserted field? Doesn't she care about herself more than that? Her children?

"Why did you agree to meet that guy in such a secluded place? That was really stupid."

*Great.* That was the wrong thing to say—at least

being so freaking blunt about it—but once the words are out, I can't take them back. Emmy's entire body stiffens.

"Who the hell are you to tell me what to do? I had the situation under control."

"The hell you did. You were arguing with a man with a gun."

"I didn't have a choice."

Tears spring from her eyes like geysers. *Well, shit.*

I lean toward Emmy and place my hand on hers. Shocks of electricity shoot through my fingers. *What the hell?* My hand jerks away. Emmy's intake of breath tells me she felt it, too. I lower my hand again slowly, this time anticipating the contact, and again cover her hand with mine. The electricity still hums between us.

"I know it's none of my business. I just can't get the picture of you staring down the barrel of a gun out of my head."

"Me either." She sniffles. The tip of her nose is red. I release the grip I have on her hand and give her another napkin.

"I'll ask again. Why did you meet that guy? Do you really need the money that badly?"

"Unfortunately, my mortgage is due soon, plus a few other things, and I need money. I'm selling things to make ends meet." She looks away, embarrassed to admit the truth. "My jerk of a husband, well ex-husband, made sure his expensive lawyer gave him the best deal in our divorce settlement. I'm just trying to hold out long enough to graduate in August. Then, hopefully, I can get a job that will support me and my kids."

"Isn't there child support or alimony?"

"Not enough. Andrew says that I can make due on what he gives me if I move to an apartment. That's a stretch. I will end up there soon enough, and that's fine, but I'm trying to give my kids one last summer in their house, in the neighborhood where they grew up. Once I graduate, I'm hoping to get a job that pays enough for us to at least buy a townhouse. I want the kids to be able to stay in the same schools, but the area where we live doesn't have many townhouses, and even fewer condos, or apartments. I want to give them this time, even if it means selling jewelry to do it. I don't need fancy things. Besides, the bracelet was a five-year wedding anniversary gift. It's not like I want it anymore."

"You've sold more than just the bracelet?"

"I did this one other time, and it worked perfectly. I sold a diamond pendent necklace that my father-in-law gave me as a wedding gift. Didn't want that anymore either, and the proceeds subsidized two months of mortgage."

"How many children do you have?"

She smiles a weak smile. "Two."

"That's what I thought, Hayes and Audrey?"

Her eyes widen and flash with anger. *Tread lightly here.*

"How did you know that?"

"The stickers on the back of your van. You really shouldn't advertise such details for everyone to see. Just from the information on your car, I can tell that Audrey does cheerleading at WDC. I don't know what that is, but I can look it up on the Internet quick enough. Hayes likes swim and is on the Millbrook Marlins swim team." Her face turns sour again. "Look, don't shoot the messenger. I'm just regurgitating the information that you advertise to everyone on the back of your own car."

"Hayes just turned fifteen, and Audrey's twelve. Andrew turned out to be a jerk of a husband, but he gave me two beautiful children." She shifts in her seat and turns toward me, her hands folded in her lap. "Look, I know that I'm not handling this well. It's just that I'm not the needy type. I'm used to taking care of everything myself. I don't know what to do."

I lean closer and place my hand on top of her folded ones. She doesn't pull away. My hand hums where it touches hers.

"You don't have to do anything. Just tell me where I need to drive you."

She tilts her head upwards. Her eyes meet mine, glistening from the tears she's cried. It takes all the self-control that I have not to lean in farther and kiss her. Instead, I give her hands one last squeeze and turn to face the steering wheel.

"Where are we going?" She gives me the first part of the directions, and I pull back onto the main road.

"Are you married?" *Does she wants to know if I'm single, or is she just making conversation?*

"I was once, but I'm not anymore."

"Divorced?"

"Yeah."

"Any children?"

*Crap.*

"No."

"Did you like being a SEAL? I mean you must have since you did it for twenty years. It's just so amazing."

"It was great for a while, but as you can imagine, it's hard on the body. It's not the job for an old man like me."

"You're hardly old. Besides, if I admit that you're old, then I would have to admit that I am, too."

*She is not old.*

"Old for a SEAL, I guess. No one can say that you're old." Our eyes meet again, and we share a smile. I already love to see her smile. Need to get in as many as I can before she gets out of my truck.

"Tell me about it. What kind of work did you do?"

"I was with SEAL Team Four and responsible for technical surveillance. We do most of our work in Central and South America. I can't really talk about more than that."

She nods. "So I guess the cyber security thing makes sense then, and your fluency in Spanish." I shrug. "And your ability to take out two gun-wielding criminals all by yourself. That really was amazing."

We share another smile.

"Was it amazing enough to get you to go out to dinner with me?"

Smile gone. Eyes wide with panic. *Not a good sign.*

"I guess that's a *no* then. What does a guy have to do to get a date around here?"

"I'm sorry. It's not that I wouldn't like to. You see, my kids have a swim meet tonight. I'm trying to make it to the pool in time to see them warm up. Then I have class, and then you're leaving town."

"Class? What kind of class are you taking?"

And let's see how quickly and comfortably she answers my question. Is she just telling me a story so she doesn't have to out with me?

"I'm finishing my Bachelor's degree in finance. I'm taking my last class, Corporate Financial Study, and then I'm done. Only three more weeks. I should be counting the days I guess, at this point. Then I will have time to look for a real job and move on with my life."

*Sounds like a legitimate answer.*

"We're here. Turn right at the next stoplight."

We turn into her neighborhood. A whistle involuntarily leaves my lips.

## Chapter Ten

### Emmy

Our neighborhood is gated, and since my car and access key are now miles away, I give Jackson directions to stay to the left to speak with the guard.

"Do you feel safe living here?"

"Sure. They are really strict about who they let in."

Jackson doesn't say anything else, but it does seem like he wants to. His mouth is pressed tightly as if it takes some effort to keep his opinion to himself.

Luckily, the guard on duty is Carter. He walks to the truck to speak with Jackson about entry. He looks very handsome in his suit. Sweat is evident on his forehead, but he would never dream of taking off his suit jacket. Carter's guarded the gate here for years, and he takes his job very seriously. He's always been one of the nicest people in the neighborhood. Of course, he isn't even technically in the neighborhood, and that in itself says a lot about where I live.

Carter is immediately all smiles and even gives me a thumbs up when he thinks Jackson isn't looking, although I'm pretty sure that Jackson saw him do it. Carter hasn't been stealthy about anything since he hit his sixties, and that was around ten years ago. I've made Carter's day by bringing a man here. He's been after me to date for more than a year, something I definitely don't have time for.

We thank Carter, and I give Jackson directions to the swimming pool. "You can just drop me off there, and I'll walk home and then get a ride to class with a friend."

"Or, you could let me drive you to class. Carter seems like a very intelligent man, and he approves of me." Jackson's smile is beaming. I knew he saw Carter. "Maybe you should skip class and let me take you out to dinner after all."

"I can't skip class. It's compressed in the summer, and that would be the equivalent of missing three regular classes."

"Okay. Well, I guess this is goodbye again."

"I guess so. Thank you for everything."

My legs are shaky as they hit the asphalt, but

they steady as I move through the open gate and the throng of people preparing and waiting for the swim meet to begin. The tall tree line just outside the fence shades the pool area this time of the day. *Thank goodness.* I need somewhat of a break. A deep breath escapes my lungs. My fingers grasp the chain link fence for support. Another deep breath. *I can do this.*

Hayes stands at the far corner of the pool deck, chatting with a group of his friends. Audrey and her best friend Becca are in line at the snack bar. I think she uses the meets as a chance to pig out on junk food. Somehow she manages to eat like a pig and still swim well. I wouldn't be able to keep it down.

"Bad day?" Anne hands me a Diet Coke. The metal of the can freezes my fingers.

"Got any rum to go in this?"

"That bad, huh?"

"Worse. No time to get into it though. Thanks for taking care of Hayes and Audrey...again. You're a life saver."

Anne grins. "I know." Her eyes widen as her grin slowly fades. Her face is turning pink.

"What's wrong? Are you sick?"

"Nothing. Oh crap. He's coming over."

"Who's coming over?"

I turn to see Jackson walking towards me carrying my purse. My eyes roll, and I do a mental head slap. He smiles and waves. Anne all but swoons.

"You know him? Why does he have your purse? Is *he* the reason you were late? I will gladly watch your children any time day or night if it means you get to be with him."

"It's not what it looks like."

"Why not? He's hot." She gets her whispers in just before Jackson arrives.

"Hey. You forgot your purse in my truck."

My hand reaches outward and wraps around the leather straps.

"Thanks. Sorry about that. You probably had to park three blocks away. Parking is always insane whenever there's a meet."

"Four blocks, but who's counting." His mouth slowly spreads into a grin. My throat feels tight, but I manage a smile.

"I'm Anne." She speaks quickly through her enormous grin. She extends her hand, and Jackson shakes it.

"Very nice to meet you, Anne. You must be a good friend to Emmy. Thanks for helping her out since she was tied up."

Anne smiles an all too knowing smile. Why did Jackson have to say *tied up?* Now I'm going to have to explain to Anne that I was not actually tied up. *Is it suddenly warmer out here?* She knows that I wouldn't do anything like that, but she will still enjoy teasing the crap out of me about it. Then there will be mental images. *Help me.*

"See you later, Emmy. Nice to meet you, Jackson."

Just like that, we're alone. Well, alone except for the many pairs of eyes that I feel watching us. My neck prickles with the realization. It's not like Jackson blends in here. *Good.* This will give the pool rats something to talk about.

*Something to talk about, indeed.* Marci Fernico comes running over to us. *This is different.* Marci hasn't even waved to me in over a year, and now she's tripping over herself to get to me—well, let's be real—*to Jackson,* before anyone else. I take his arm when I see her and her embarrassing cleavage and bleach blond hair coming our way.

*Holy muscles!* Jackson's arm is huge. He smiles down at me.

"Emmy! I haven't seen you in so long."

*You have actually. You just chose to ignore me.* She bats her heavily mascaraed eyelashes.

"How have you been?"

Of course, she isn't even looking at me. She's staring at Jackson like he's a juicy steak. Well, he kind of is. Even in my current state of nun-ness, I can appreciate looking at him. He isn't GQ gorgeous. He's more rugged than that, more like someone you would find on the cover of *Men's Health*. I smile my best smile.

"Oh, hello, Marci. I've been wonderful." *Yes, Marci, read whatever meaning you want to in my choice of the word "wonderful."* "This is my friend Jackson." *You can read whatever you want into the meaning of "friend" as well.* Jackson shakes her hand politely.

Marci looks like she's going to spontaneously combust.

"Well, Marci, we need to be moving along. We need to wish Hayes and Audrey good luck."

I hug Jackson's arm even tighter.

"Good to meet you, Marci."

She literally giggles like a little girl before turning and walking back toward her friends.

"What the heck was that?" I pull him away from Marci toward Hayes's group. "Guess I can see why you don't like her."

"What do you mean?" *Is it that obvious?* "If you like Marci with her spray-on tan and big fake boobs, you go for it."

"You can't be serious. Marci's ridiculous, and her boobs aren't the only fake thing about her. Am I right?"

"Yeah. She's one of the pool rats."

"The what?"

"That's my nickname for them—the women in the neighborhood who think they're too good to speak to just anyone. They all sit together over there under that umbrella and talk about everyone else." We look towards the group just as Marci is joining them. They're all staring at us. "It's just like high school all over again."

\*\*\*

"Hey, Mom."

*Hayes.* He stands a few feet away, the corners of his lips turn upward to form a shy smile. *Shoot. He saw us.* I slip my arm from Jackson's. I haven't made any effort to date since the divorce, so it only makes sense that Hayes is curious about what's happening here.

"He can't know what I've been through today." The words are barely a whisper as they leave my mouth. I narrow my eyes as well to help Jackson understand. My children can't know that I was held at gunpoint. They also don't need to know that I was trying to sell my jewelry to make ends meet.

"Hi, sweetie."

I close the distance between us and place my hand on Hayes's bare shoulder. The curiosity evident in his brown eyes makes me want to pull him to me, but I don't dare initiate the move that Hayes would define as his social suicide. I haven't been allowed to hug him in public since he was in the fourth grade. Sure he's almost six-feet tall now—that's eight inches taller than me—but he's pretty skinny, and he's still my baby.

"Hayes, this is my *friend*, Jackson." *This time I really mean friend.* "Jackson, this is my son, Hayes." Bless his heart, Jackson stands still for a moment as Hayes studies him. Hayes's brain is clearly working overtime to process exactly what is going on here between us. Hayes steps forward and shakes Jackson's hand. Pride shoots through me. My Hayes is intelligent, good-looking, funny, and to top it all off, he has manners.

"How do you know my mom?" *And Hayes is also very protective of me.*

I don't give Jackson a chance to answer. "I met Jackson earlier today. Then, when I had a little car trouble, he offered to give me a ride here."

Hayes's eyes are harder now, assessing first Jackson and then me. Is it that obvious that I'm lying, or does Hayes just suspect there's more to the story?

"Are you in the Navy or something?"

*Good.* Hayes has noticed Jackson's shirt and we are gladly moving on to a new subject.

Jackson shifts his weight and smiles at Hayes. Jackson's happy about the change of subject, too.

"I was a SEAL—well, technically I guess I still am since my retirement isn't official for another month."

Hayes's entire face lights up. He fires off question after question. Jackson appears to be much more comfortable discussing his missions than his relationship with me. *Me, too.* They are quickly in deep conversation only to be interrupted briefly when I introduce Jackson to Audrey. She says a quick *hello* and then disappears with her friends. She's just as curious as Hayes, but she is more of a watch from afar type, which she does. She joins her friends but barely takes her eyes off of us.

As fun as it is to be here with them, I do have to get to class. My friend, Leah, is already on her way to pick me up, and there's no way I'm leaving a practical stranger here semi-alone with my kids. We both wish Hayes luck and wave goodbye to Audrey before Jackson walks me back to the parking lot. This time we exchange phone numbers as part of our goodbye. I can't imagine ever calling him, but it's too awkward not to get his number at this point. It's a better goodbye than the first time. I'm trying not to look like I'm running away, but I kind of am. I admit it. Sure I need to get to class, but I also need to get away from Jackson so that I can process all that has happened to me today.

"Do you have a recommendation for a hotel? Maybe somewhere that has a good restaurant?"

"Is that just so you can take Marci out to dinner?" My tone is teasing—I think—but what the heck am I doing asking that question out loud? It's reasonable that he would ask for a hotel recommendation, and it's certainly none of my business even if Marci was his purpose for asking, which I'm sure it's not. It would just really tick me off if he saw Marci again. I know that men prefer a tall blonde with gigantic boobs to a short brunette with practically no boobs. *At least mine are real. Ha!* Sure, I turned Jackson down for dinner when he asked me, but damn it if Marci's allowed to get her claws into him. Prickles of embarrassment crawl up my neck.

Jackson smiles a devilish grin.

"You're onto me."

*Please let him be kidding.*

*Please God, anyone but Marci.*

Jackson gives me a quick peck on the cheek. Now

the prickles of heat travel from my neck clear up to my forehead.

"Are you going to be okay?"

"Of course." I try to smile, but I know it's weak. "I hope I didn't delay your trip too much."

"Not at all. I'll probably find a place to stay around here for tonight and then leave sometime in the morning, whenever Detective Marshall gives me the go-ahead."

"Thanks for everything."

"Goodbye, Emmy."

"Goodbye."

I look into those blue eyes one last time and then run to meet Leah, my ride to class. If I would allow myself to admit it, it's disappointing that Jackson is leaving right away. Once all the craziness stopped, it was nice talking with him. Of course, maybe I just feel that way because it's safe. He's leaving, so there's no pressure, and I don't have to worry about what might have been.

## *Chapter Eleven*

### *Jackson*

"Dammit, Smitty. Answer your fucking phone!"

What the hell? Has he just dropped off the face of the earth? I disconnect the call...again. Must be the tenth time I've tried to call him today. Despite his claims to the contrary, my sixth sense tells me that he's up to something. The tightness in my gut doesn't lie. The feeling is even stronger now that I can't get in touch with him.

He should be at home right now, sleeping. Apparently, no one is home because no one answered the door. Not surprising since there was no car in the driveway, but there should have been. This situation deserves to be examined a little further. He's my friend, and after everything that's happened, I need to look out for him.

My meeting this morning with Detective Marshall was quick and painless. He asked me a few more questions about the events that took place yesterday, and I signed some papers. He had a few questions to ask about my past criminal record, but really not many considering the trouble Smitty got me into. Of course, the charges were dropped in that case, so maybe there's really not much to talk about there. The truth is the truth, and that's all I've ever told about anything. It's just that the truth doesn't always paint a story that's black and white.

The questioning didn't take long though, probably because Detective Marshall had already called just about everyone I know to corroborate my information. That's what it feels like anyway. I've received two calls from friends letting me know that the thorough detective has been checking up on my character. My last commanding officer was called. He's a talker, so I'm sure word of my incident will spread, and there will be more calls to come.

I can't leave Williamsburg without being sure that everything's on the up-and-up with Smitty. Or, is Emmy the real reason that I don't want to leave? Either way, I'm definitely not finished here yet.

## Chapter Twelve

*Emmy*

My eyes blink and take in my surroundings. My office. *Great.* Another daydream. I wiggle the mouse to wake up my computer...again. I'm just about useless today. A whoosh of breath escapes as I try in vain to study the spreadsheet in front of me. *Not gonna happen.* Jackson has dominated my thoughts since I left him last night at the pool, just like his blue eyes dominated my dreams.

My thoughts are not only of Jackson. I remember all too well that I still have the same problem that I had yesterday. My mortgage is due in a week, and I still don't have the money to pay it. My plan to sell the bracelet was a big flop. Even if I felt comfortable using Craig's List for this again, which I'm not sure that I do, there haven't been any other offers to buy the bracelet. How am I going to get the money to pay my bills?

Hayes talked of Jackson nonstop this morning. He came right out and asked if Jackson and I were *hanging out*. Is that fifteen year old code for dating? He and Audrey both seemed disappointed with my answer. Somehow, I felt disappointed with my answer, too.

*That sure was quick.*

It doesn't matter, though. Jackson is gone. That fact alone is probably what is allowing me to admit to myself that I liked him. *Geez.* Amazing deep blue eyes and a body that's hard as a rock. What's not to like? Plus, I only knew him for a couple hours. That's not enough time to get to know a person well enough to be disappointed by them. So, of course I like him.

And I don't feel guilty for Googling Jackson. I'm not an idiot. I don't know anyone whom I can ask to do a background check, but an internet search is the next best thing. As expected, Jackson is a hero. There were two hits about commendations he received, and he was also involved in the organizing of a big charity run to raise money for ALS.

I've thought about calling him, but what would be the point? He's probably well on his way to Nashville by now, or who knows where. It's silly for me to brood about this all day. I have my life and my family to care for. Someday, in the future, when I finish school, get a job, and move to wherever we're going, I might have time to date. Just not now, so stop pining. Men are not in my plan right now and won't be for a long time to come.

The kids and I went through our normal summer routine this morning. I prepared their breakfast, made their lunches, and then dropped them off at the pool for swim practice. During that time, Hayes asked me way too many questions.

How did I meet Jackson? I had to fib the answer on that one. Hayes now thinks that I met Jackson when my car got a flat tire. I really hate lying to him, but I can't tell my children that Jackson saved me from two men with guns. *Boy, wouldn't Hayes think that was awesome?*

Hayes and Audrey both say that they're ready for me to have a man in my life, but I don't think they would be so easy going about it if ever confronted with the reality, at least any time soon. Their father is remarried, and somehow they're okay with that. Whenever the possibility of me dating has even come up in the past, even in jest, they've clearly been unhappy about it. What's different about this time? It's Jackson. He's had quite the effect on all of us.

Summer break has just started, and I can already feel the boredom. They have swim team practice every morning. They hang out at the pool for a couple of hours with their friends afterwards and then go hang out at their friends' houses in the afternoon. Sometimes they all come to our house. *That's a lot of hanging out.* I used to be home for them in the summer. We would go on day trips and find other fun things to do. I used to be there for them every day after school, too. That's not our reality anymore. They're latchkey kids because mommy has to work now and just when Hayes is at the age to get into trouble. Boys really do need to have a man around to look up to. I try really hard, but it's just not the same. Lord knows that his father isn't there for him consistently.

*Whoa!* Don't start thinking about that today. My brain is too full already to bring Andrew into this. I sigh heavily and look back at my spreadsheet... again. Thank goodness it's almost time to go home.

Hope comes by my desk at four o'clock. I sit up and give her a big smile, but I can tell by the way she studies me that she isn't buying my efforts to look normal. I've been able to get away with being zoned out because Hope's been out of our office for most of the day attending meetings.

"Emmy, may I speak to you in my office for a few moments, please?"

Carla, who sits nearby, looks up from her computer but doesn't say anything as I stand and follow Hope into her office. I plop down in one of the chairs reserved for visitors as Hope closes the door behind me.

"What's going on? Spill it." She sits down behind

her large wooden desk and looks at me with curious eyes. That's the good and bad part of having a best friend—can't get anything past them.

"Something happened yesterday."

*That's the understatement of the century.*

She raises her eyebrows and waits for me to continue. Another big sigh escapes. Lots of sighing going on today. I swallow, shift in my seat, and begin.

"So, yesterday I tried to sell a bracelet."

"You told me that you were going to let me come with you for these meetings. I don't want you meeting strangers by yourself."

"I know. I was in a hurry yesterday. Plus, I made the meeting place in the touristy part of town where there would be plenty of people around." *Sort-of. Not really.*

This whole situation is embarrassing. No one else needs to be involved in my mess, not even Hope. She stares back at me, her light green eyes full of understanding. If we weren't such good friends, then she wouldn't know my every thought right now. I wouldn't trade Hope's friendship for the world, but it would be nice to have some secrets at least some of the time.

"What happened?"

Another sigh. Maybe I'm oxygen deprived.

"The buyer tried to rob me."

"What?"

"These two guys were there, and they had guns. Then this other man was suddenly there. He saved me."

"Wow." Hope's eyes are huge.

"No kidding *wow*. The guy was amazing. He disarmed the men, just took them out."

"Is he hot?"

*What a question.* I nod, a knowing smile on my lips.

"So hot."

*Speaking of hot, is it getting warmer in here?*

"When do you see him again?"

And my smile fades.

"He's gone. On his way to California."

"No. I'm so sorry."

"It's for the best. I don't have time to date anyone now anyway."

"Sounds like you'd be willing to make time for this guy. You haven't even looked at a man other than Andrew for almost twenty years. This one must be pretty special." *Crap. She's right.* "Is that what someone has to do to get your attention? Save you from armed gunmen?"

My lips curl up into a grin.

"Maybe."

"Whatever. It's close enough to quitting time. Why don't you get out of here? Next time you try one of your illicit transactions, I want to be there. Promise?"

"We'll see."

"I mean it, Emmy."

"Okay. Okay."

Hope can be so stubborn. But, then, so can I. Maybe that's why we get each other so well. I met Hope when I was an undergrad, just before I met Andrew. We both thought we were really something back then—young and free. We were going to take on the world together. I guess we did in our own way. It's just not the way that we planned to do it back then.

\*\*\*

One last thing before I leave for the day. I take a moment to check my personal e-mail, something I've been too preoccupied to think about much.

Ms. Bennett,

I waited for you for a full hour this morning, and you never showed up. I accommodated your time change, but honestly, I don't like waiting. Have you changed your mind, or were you delayed? I would still like to buy your bracelet. Please let me know if it is still for sale.

Gerald Lehman

I suck in a deep breath and grab onto the edge of my desk. This morning? The meeting was set up for three-thirty yesterday afternoon. I never changed the time. I click the *Sent Mail* icon and hold my breath. There's no correspondence there showing that the time of our meeting was changed. I've been busy lately, but there's no way I could forget something this important.

I retrieve Detective Marshall's business card from my purse and dial his number with shaky fingers.

"Perfect timing, Ms. Bennet. I was just about to call you."

"Really? Why?"

"To see if you can drop by the station to review and sign a statement about what happened yesterday. The two assailants have been identified as Jose Martinez and Manuel Castro. Have you heard of them?"

"No. Never."

"Both have a history of petty theft, nothing ever involving a firearm, only very small stuff. They are still in jail and may be for a while. The judge set their bail higher than usual because of their escalation to using a firearm. Their families do not have a lot of money, but they will probably make bail eventually. Neither has shared much information with us so far. We're still working on them."

*Working on them?* That doesn't sound good. Images of water boarding come to mind.

"I called because I have some new information to share with you. I just read an email from the real Mr. Lehman asking why I didn't show up to meet him today. It looks like the men you have in custody hacked my email account and sent the real Mr. Lehman a revised meeting time so that they could meet with me instead."

I relay all the pertinent details like my e-mail address and password so that he can log into my account himself.

"I will give this information to our IT specialists so that they can research what happened, but it does sound like your account was most likely hacked. It could have been one of the men who held you up yesterday, or it could be a third party yet to be identified."

*There might be more.*

"We will let you know as soon as we hear something. In the meantime, you need to be very careful. These two are behind bars, but we don't know who else may be involved in this."

*A chill travels down my spine.*

"Can I come by now and sign the papers? I'm leaving work in a few minutes."

*Do not ask him if Jackson has signed his papers already.*

"Now is perfect."

I practically run out of the building and start speed walking towards my car. I just want to be home. The heat is just as oppressive as yesterday.

This has been the longest workday, yet I've accomplished the least amount of work ever, and now I have this new news to worry about.

Tomorrow is a new day, and I'll be back on track then. Tonight, I'm going to make hot dogs and baked beans for dinner—Audrey's favorite and a meal within my budget—and stay in with my family. Maybe I'll postpone my studying until later tonight so that we can watch a movie together. *Yep. Family time is just what I need.* I smile to myself as I walk to my car.

## Chapter Thirteen

## *Jackson*

Carter is the guard on duty again today. Makes things much easier for me. This was the one weak part of my plan. There are ways to get past guards like this one. Shoot, worst case, all I'd have to do is park and then walk inside, but my plan will have more of an impact this way. Emmy declined my dinner invitation last night. Sure, she had school to use as an excuse, but she would have declined anyway. Plus, this plan kills two birds with one stone. I get to see Emmy again, and I can give her a lesson in personal security. I don't want to leave tomorrow and worry about her.

Not only does Carter let me in, he's thrilled to see me. It's obvious that he thinks a lot of Emmy, and why not? She's a good person. Whereas that Marci woman from the swim meet was fake on many levels, Emmy is *real.*

I pull my truck into her driveway and wait. Will Emmy be upset to see me here? Definitely. I just hope that I can explain before she kicks me out.

# Chapter Fourteen

## Emmy

The stop at the police station is quick. *Thank goodness*. Never want to go back there for any reason. The visit reminds me of the nightmares I have sometimes about Hayes being in jail. He hangs with a good crowd, but I'm a mom, and moms worry.

The drive home is accomplished today without any issues although the sight of the shopping center where I careened off the road yesterday makes me wince. Jackson scared the crap out of me when he opened my car door. My first thought at seeing him was *stalker*, but his eyes quickly changed my mind. Those expressive blue eyes of his were full of understanding.

*Stop thinking about him.* That's easier said than done.

Carter is on duty again. I wave to him as I drive through the resident gate. It opens for me automatically with my access key, so I don't stop to speak with him. He'd have too many questions— evident by the silly and knowing smile on his face. I don't have enough energy today for that conversation.

I kept up with the location of my children via text messages throughout the day. I pull into the driveway at the home of Hayes's friend, Matt and give a wave as Hayes climbs into the car. Next, we drive to Audrey's friend Hillary's house. Audrey's not ready to leave, but after just a little whining and one threat from me, she gets into the car. My hope for a family night is becoming a reality. Happy feelings spread through me in anticipation of the fun evening ahead of us. This is just what I need, but my kids have to cooperate. They sometimes feel they are too old and too cool for family night.

*Happy feelings gone.*

Why is Jackson's truck parked in my driveway?

How is Jackson's truck parked in my driveway? He shouldn't have been able to get through the guard gate without my permission? No wonder Carter had such a big smile on his face.

Why isn't Jackson heading off into the sunset? I've been thinking good thoughts about him all day, but those thoughts are now gone. *Crap.* Maybe he really is a stalker. Big sigh. I knew he was too good to be true.

"Looks like we have company. Whose truck is that?"

"I think that it might be Jackson's."

Hayes's entire face lights up. "Really? I thought you said he was gone. This is awesome!"

I pull into the driveway and look toward the cab of the truck. Jackson looks back at me. Do my eyes reflect the panic now thumping through my body?

*What is he doing here?*

Hayes hops out of my van before I even get it into park.

"Hayes! Get back here. You need to stay in the van until I figure out why Jackson's here."

"Oh, Mom, don't be so dramatic." He grumbles, but he does return to his seat.

"Just let me speak with Jackson first and make sure everything's okay."

Audrey isn't as excited. Her face is pensive; her mouth forms a tight line. I force a smile onto my face just for her. She doesn't need to worry—*I don't think.*

This is ridiculous. An hour ago, I was sad that he had left town. He's here now. I should be thrilled, but instead, I'm a nervous wreck. Jackson climbs out of his truck as I walk toward him. As I do, my nervousness is quickly taken over with anger. By the time I reach him, I'm borderline furious.

"What the hell are you doing here?"

"I just wanted to see you again."

"I'm calling the police."

"To tell them what, that I came over to make you dinner?"

The vision of him laughing with the police officers yesterday pops into my mind. They almost seemed to enjoy sharing their little guy time. Detective Patterson showed no reaction and didn't even seem to care. Is that what would happen if I called them today? Add frustration to the mix.

## Chapter Fifteen

### Jackson

Yeah, Emmy's good and mad. Not a surprise. Maybe that's what she needs for my message to sink into her hard head.

This probably isn't the time to tell her how gorgeous she looks when she's angry, but boy, does she. Her face is flushed, and her brown eyes emit a yellow glow that makes them look like they're on fire. I do care about Emmy's safety—I do—so hopefully, that will come across in my explanation. I have to admit that just showing up at her house is a low blow, but she needs to take her safety seriously.

"I know another shock after yesterday's scare is not a friendly thing, but I just want to prove to you how easily someone can get into your neighborhood. Most gated communities are a joke, and yours is no exception. The guards might harass a few people here and there, but if a criminal wants to get in, he will."

"How did you get in?"

"I told Carter the truth. I told him that I wanted to surprise you with dinner, and he let me in willingly. He wants you to be happy and apparently, if that means letting a stranger in, so be it."

"You took advantage of an old man?"

"I just told him the truth, but there are other ways I could have gotten in. I could have flashed a fake badge or business card. It's a piece of cake. Besides, if I didn't have any other options, I could have just walked in. They let anyone walk in."

Her eyes are wide and thoughtful. "How did you know which house was mine?"

My eyes roll involuntarily.

"A two second internet search told me your address and phone number. A seven-year-old could do that."

"It's a safe neighborhood. We've never had any trouble."

"Then you've been lucky. I only did this to make a point. You need to be more careful."

Emmy's gaze meets mine as she weighs the truthfulness of my comments. I hope that I've thrown her off enough to actually teach her a lesson about this stuff. She shouldn't be meeting strangers in a secluded place, and she shouldn't have stickers on her van advertising her children's names and activities. She needs to take her family's safety more seriously. This is just common sense.

"Who made you my guardian angel?"

"Mom, is everything okay?" Hayes steps closer. Emmy turns to him.

"I thought I told you to wait in the car."

The regret is clear on Emmy's face. Hayes looks visibly flustered.

"Sorry, Mom. I was worried. You look upset." Hayes looks from his mom to me. He stands straighter. "Is everything okay out here?"

Hayes asks the question of Emmy, but his eyes never leave me. He stands ramrod straight and stares at me with brown eyes definitely inherited from Emmy. He couldn't hurt me, but the determination on his face clearly shows that he would do anything to protect his mother.

"It's okay, Hayes." I keep my voice soft and even, backing down from Hayes's unspoken challenge. "I just want to make dinner for you all, steak and potatoes on the grill. I even brought stuff for a salad. Is that okay, Emmy?"

Hayes and I both look at Emmy. His expression morphs from challenging to begging. Emmy sighs.

"Of course. Hayes, please tell your sister that Jackson is staying for dinner tonight."

A *yippee* escapes from Hayes's lips as he turns and motions to Audrey. Jackson walks directly to me and places his hand on my shoulder.

"I'm sorry, Emmy. I know that coming here like this was a bit underhanded. I wanted to make a point, and I realize now that I went too far. I hope you can understand and forgive me."

"I get it. I do. Just please don't sneak in the neighborhood like this again. Stop and talk to Carter and follow the visitation protocols. This is our home, and you have to respect that."

"Of course. Now let me get you a beer. Do you like beer?"

"Yes, and thank you. I could really use one."

***

Hayes grabs a load of the groceries I brought and starts toward the front door. All that's left for me to carry is the beer. I grab the handle and follow Emmy and her family up the walkway. Hayes transfers the plastic sacks to one hand as he reaches the door and then just turns the doorknob and walks inside the house. The door was unlocked.

*Unlocked.*

*Sonofabitch.* How can she leave her front door unlocked? I've been lecturing her on how to keep her family safe, and it never occurred to me that she would be this foolish. Deep breathes help to calm me, but only a little.

"Do you mean to tell me that I could have just walked right into your house? Granted, I could have gotten in if I'd wanted to. It isn't hard. You probably have a key hidden out here somewhere. Am I right?" Emmy looks down at her feet. "An alarm might have stopped me, but if you have one, you definitely aren't using it. You have to do better than this to take care of yourself and your family."

"The kids leave the door unlocked during the day because some days they run in and out a lot. Nothing has ever happened."

"You've been lucky."

"We'll be more careful from now on. Now, give me the damn beer you promised me. I think I'm going to need more than one."

My stern look dissolves as my lips move into a smile involuntarily. I could really like this woman.

Emmy holds the door open for me, and I step inside onto the white marble tile of the foyer. A low whistle escapes. *Wow!* A grand staircase curves up in front of me. My eyes follow it up, and I notice the large crystal chandelier above me. I follow Emmy toward the back of the house, taking it all in as I go. Each room is decorated nicely. The furniture is high quality for sure, a big departure from the stuff I bought at that discount place. I don't know rugs, but the ones that lay in each room look very expensive.

The large cherry table in the dining room seats ten. *Ten*. My own dinette set seats four, and I certainly don't have a matching buffet or the china cabinet that takes up an entire wall. But then I've never lived in a house large enough to hold a dining set this large.

Despite all of the richness here, the house somehow manages to have a lived-in look. Family photos are placed around the rooms. A crocheted blanket lies rumpled on one side of the sofa. And, the thin layer of dust in some areas tells me that there isn't a cleaning person who visits here regularly. I'd bet most everyone else in this neighborhood can afford a maid.

We find Hayes and Audrey in the kitchen unloading the groceries I brought onto the large, granite countertop. They finish and then both look at me as if awaiting their next order, so I give them one. Audrey begins preparing the salad. Hayes shows me to the grill. I've never had kitchen helpers like this before, but they couldn't be more eager to help.

## Chapter Sixteen

*Emmy*

Hayes and Audrey help with dinner whenever I ask them, but this level of participation is unprecedented. And they work with smiles on their faces. A dinner of salad, steak, and grilled potatoes is completed in no time. The scent of the succulent steak hits me hard. It's been forever since we've had steak. We make our plates buffet-style and then sit together at the kitchen table.

Question after question is thrust at Jackson. *Were you ever in a gunfight? Did you go on secret missions? Did you ever get to fire a rocket launcher? Do you have any weapons in your truck?* Fortunately, Jackson wasn't able to answer many of their questions, or at least that's what he told them. Answers would just lead to more questions, and it would never end.

Finally Jackson turns the questions back on the kids. He asks about school, their friends, swim team, and all the rest until dinner is over, and both Hayes and Audrey are all talked out. They excuse themselves to go upstairs and take showers. They actually just want to run away before they're roped into doing the dishes, but I let them go. Jackson needs a break.

The kid-free silence fills the air.

"Your children are amazing,"

"Thank you. I think so, but it's nice to hear someone else agree."

"Since you cooked, I'll clean up the kitchen."

Jackson moves to protest, but I give him the mom eye, and he backs down.

"At least let me clear the table."

"Deal."

I work at the sink, rinsing the dishes that Jackson brings me and then loading them into the dishwasher. The work is quick, partly because I have a partner and partly because the meal was grilled, so no pots and pans were harmed in the making of this dinner.

"Everything was really delicious. Thank you for cooking. If you feel so inclined to cook for us again, just let me know, and I'll leave word with Carter."

"As long as I can grill it, I can cook it. But, that's all I can do."

"Well, you're good at it."

I smile and turn back to the sink. The kitchen is just about clean.

*What happens next?*

*Will he leave? For good this time?*

Every pore of my body tingles as I feel Jackson move to me. My eyes stay focused on the faucet, but my body feels that he's there behind me. I place my hands on the counter to brace myself. Jackson matches my movements and places his large, manly hands on top of mine as he brackets me against the counter, his arms touch mine from our shoulders down to our hands. His lips are so close to my skin. He whispers only a single word.

"Emmy."

His breath travels over my ear. This one tickling breath causes a shiver to travel from my ear down to my toes. My stomach lurches. Just one word and my insides turn to mush.

"Why did you stay?"

My throat is so tight that the words are barely a whisper. Jackson leans his head down and gently kisses my bare shoulder next to the strap of my tank top. Is it possible for all the blood in my body to rush to my shoulder? That's what it feels like as my head becomes light and my knees weak.

Jackson's hands move to my shoulders. He slowly turns me around to face him. My hands find the countertop again to brace myself. Without the support, my dizziness would surely send me falling into his arms again. *That wouldn't be a bad thing, but I don't want to be a fainting princess.* His body is so close to mine, not touching me, but so close that I can feel his energy pulling me to him.

He cups my chin and tilts it up toward his so that our eyes connect.

"Do you want me to leave?" His blue eyes darken.

*No.* "Yes."

"Mo-om!"

*Thank goodness for the warning call.*

Jackson stumbles away from me as I turn around to face the sink to hide my already blushing skin. *Look busy.* I turn the water on and quickly spray the sink. Jackson opens the refrigerator. Hayes walks into the kitchen. I turn my head towards him. *Look nonchalant. You're just doing the dishes. Nothing to see here.*

"Mom, can I go down to the club and hit the weight room?"

*The weight room, huh? Guess I know what's behind this.* I have to clear my thickened throat to speak.

"Sure, honey, just don't be too late."

"Jackson, do you want to come with me? Show me the ropes?"

Jackson closes the fridge, two beers in his hands. A mischievous smile plays on his lips.

"Maybe some other time."

Hayes shrugs, says a quick goodbye, and walks through the door to the garage and his bicycle.

# Chapter Seventeen

## *Jackson*

Funny. I feel like a teenager who just got busted, instead of the other way around. I hand Emmy a beer.

"That was a close one." A huge smile erupts on my face. "I'd forgotten everything but you."

Emmy returns my smile with a blush. A nervous giggle escapes from her throat. My arms move around her and kiss her lightly on the top of her head.

*There is just something about this woman.*

"Well, isn't this *cozy*?"

Emmy immediately tenses as we both turn towards the archway that leads from the kitchen to the dining room. A man stands there. He's blond and good-looking in a classic kind of way, like he looks his best photographed next to his yacht. But, his smarmy expression and arrogant stance tell me all that I need to know about him. I look to Emmy for guidance as to how to handle the situation. It's clear that she's unhappy that this guy is here, too. It's not much of a leap to guess that this is her ex-husband.

Emmy braces her palms on my arms in a *stay-put* gesture and turns toward the man.

"I've told you before. You can't just walk in here. You don't live here anymore."

He takes a few steps into the kitchen, his long face drawn up in a sneer, his blue eyes triumphantly looking from Emmy to me and back again. *There's no way that I'm staying put.* I step toward him and hold out my hand for a handshake. He studies my outstretched hand, and after a few seconds of inspection, slowly shakes it.

"Andrew Jacob Bennett, III." He speaks confidently, enunciating every syllable. *What an ass. Emmy was married to this guy?*

*I have a full name too—almost as long as yours, but I'm not going to give it to you.*

"Jackson."

I keep my tone polite but tighten my grip on Andrew Jacob Bennet III's hand at the same time. His smirk falters as he tries unsuccessfully to match my strength.

## Chapter Eighteen

### Emmy

Andrew always seemed tall to me at six feet. *I guess anyone seems tall to me, since I'm only five feet, two and a half inches tall.* Seeing Andrew standing next to Jackson creates a different picture. Jackson is about three inches taller, but it seems like even more. Andrew's body is toned from hours of tennis and golf. Andrew prides himself at being one of the fittest people in the club. Jackson's defined muscles make Andrew look like a dweeb. I'm definitely going to enjoy my visions of Jackson beating the crap out of him.

"Why are you here?"

He has the nerve to look smug.

"I was driving by and saw that you had company. I heard that you had *some guy* with you at the pool last night, so I stopped by to check out the situation. And what do I find, but you and this guy making out in the kitchen. Is this how you behave with my children in the house?"

"What I do in my own home is none of your damn business. My children are well cared for, and you know it. Besides, you're one to talk. Look what you and Lady Conrad were doing together in this house when we were still married."

My arms gesture wildly. My temper is barely under control, but I keep my voice as low as possible. Audrey doesn't need to hear any of this. The poor girl has heard enough fighting and crying to last her a lifetime. The telltale heat of my anger rushes up my neck to my face. *I wasn't doing anything wrong*. The gall of this guy.

"Tomorrow when you come by to pick up the kids for your visitation, you will ring the doorbell like every other visitor. Now get the hell out of *my* house, or I'm calling the police."

"There's no need to call the police." Jackson takes a step closer to Andrew. "I can take care of it."

Andrew sneers but turns and leaves in a hurry. I follow him to the front door and turn the lock ceremoniously. Jackson grabs my wrist and pulls me into his arms. My arms go around his neck to complete the embrace. His arms are strong and sure. The anger that was just shooting through me quickly subsides. My entire body comes alive with a different feeling altogether. Jackson begins planting tiny kisses on my neck, tracing a line of them up to my ear. Then his mouth finds mine. His lips are soft, but sure, and there's nothing tentative about his kiss. There's no time to mess around, we could be interrupted again. My hands move over his short hair. I pull him closer to me. His tongue explores my mouth. I was married for fifteen years, and I have never felt a kiss like this, so full of fire and passion.

But it's too much. Too much intensity. Too much feeling for someone that I just met—someone who will be out of my life as quickly as he came into it.

Breathless, I pull away and look into his now dark, smoldering eyes.

"I'm not ready for this. I'm not ready for you."

I turn away and walk quickly back to the kitchen. *I have to get away.* I grab my beer off the counter, take a long pull, and sit down at the breakfast table.

Jackson takes his beer off the counter and joins me. He sits silently for many moments, as if waiting for me to make the first move. When I don't speak, he finally does.

"So, is that what ended your marriage? He was cheating on you?"

Careful that my eyes don't meet his, I look across the room and lock onto the ceramic butterfly that Audrey made me for Mother's Day two years ago, its orange and pink wings reminding me that those were her favorite colors for the first many years of her life. In Kindergarten, she wore the same three outfits for six months since she would only wear orange and pink. We finally convinced her to wear other accent colors along with those clothes to make them last longer. She eventually grew out of it.

"Everything I do is for them."

*Which is why I never thought I would have a man in my life again.* Maybe when the kids are off in college or something, but never this soon.

Jackson scoots and resettles in his chair. "Hayes and Audrey, you mean?"

I nod. "They're what got me through it—the hell that Andrew brought to our marriage."

I swallow heavily to try to clear the thick lump from my throat.

"Things weren't great between us, but I thought that we were just in a slump. I never dreamed that he would be unfaithful. He was in bed with another woman on our fifteenth wedding anniversary."

I hear Jackson's quick intake of breath but continue with my story. If I don't get it out now, I might not be able to.

"I'd been at the spa all day getting pampered and prepped for our big dinner date. It was Andrew's idea. *Go spend the whole day at the salon. Do all that fancy stuff you women like to do. You've been married to me for fifteen years. You deserve it.*"

A large sigh escapes. I can't believe that I fell for that.

"I came home earlier than planned and found

him in our bed with Carson Conrad. She'd moved back to town after getting a divorce. She and Andrew were an item in high school. I knew that, but I didn't worry about it. She seemed so nice. I introduced Carson to other women in the neighborhood, tried to make her feel comfortable. I considered her a friend."

Jackson slides his hand across the table and interlocks it with mine. The strong hand that made Andrew wince is so gentle and comforting as it tenderly squeezes mine. My eyes travel to meet his, so dark and seductive at times, bright and mischievous at others, but now soft and caring. Jackson has the most expressive eyes I've ever seen.

"He didn't beg for my forgiveness. He didn't even say that he was sorry. He just looked up at me with this cocky expression and smiled. Then Carson smiled, and my life has never been the same. Sure I yelled and kicked them both out of the house. They just didn't seem to mind leaving. It was horrible."

"Oh, Emmy."

I shouldn't be burdening Jackson like this. I'm not even sure why I'm still talking, but I've gone this far, and I can't seem to stop.

"He moved in with her. They had been together for months before that day. I think that Andrew might have wanted me to find them together. It just seemed too easy for him."

"He's obviously a first-rate asshole, but would he do something that bad?"

"Yes. I think he would. He's always been showy. What a dramatic end to our life together."

"How were your kids when they found out?"

"Devastated. They were totally thrown. You know, when you're a child you don't notice the hints that things aren't what they should be in your family. You don't have anything to compare it to. Audrey thought that the sun and the moon orbited around Andrew. She's become very withdrawn since then. She still has some friends, but she isn't as outgoing as she was. It was bad enough that Andrew wasn't around as much for Audrey, but worse when he began spending more time with Carson's daughter. She's only a year younger than Audrey, and they go to the same school. There have been many times that Andrew has gone to school to see her performances, but he makes excuses for missing Audrey's."

*Geez. I really did marry an asshole.*

"Hayes was thirteen—a bad age to be forced to go through his parent's divorce. He was old enough to understand the enormity of what had happened. Hayes and I have become very close. One good thing that has come out of this is that Hayes treats women very well. He's taken Andrew's actions as a lesson in how *not* to treat women. The down side is that Hayes isn't a big fan of his father anymore and often tries to make plans to be unavailable on the nights and weekends that they stay with Andrew."

"Does that make Andrew angry, that Hayes

avoids him?"

"I think it did at first, but Andrew isn't so keen on his own children anymore. Well, he is, and he isn't. He wants people on the outside to see him as the perfect doting father, but he has a new family now. More than one person has dropped the hint to me that Andrew and Carson are trying to get pregnant. That would just make things perfect for them, you know."

"I'm so sorry, Emmy." I shrug my shoulders.

"He wasn't always such an ass. I came to William and Mary as a wide-eyed freshman full of ideals. I was ready to take on the world and escape from my small-town Arkansas existence at the same time. I thought I was smarter than the other girls in my town, and I wasn't going to let some cowboy knock me up and end my life. So, I worked hard and got into one of the best schools in the country. Things were going great. When I met Andrew, I thought that my life couldn't get any better. I loved him, and I knew that he loved me—at least back then he did. His family was one of the most prestigious in this town. They put up a huge fuss that he was dating white trash like me. They hated me at first. They made comments about my clothes and even my name. *So hillbilly*. Andrew stood up to them. He said he didn't care what they thought about us. He loved me."

"When I was a junior, I got pregnant. Kind of ironic, right? I leave a small town to escape the threat of a shotgun wedding and find out they have them in the big city, too."

Jackson leans forward and pulls me to him. He lightly kisses my forehead. Warmth radiates from the spot where his lips touch my skin.

"I wasn't sad though. I was happy, and so was Andrew. He even went against the wishes of his parents and named our baby Hayes instead of Andrew IV."

My lips try to curve into a wistful smile but don't quite make it.

"Andrew had already graduated and was working at an investment firm. He convinced me to drop out of school, and we got married. I became a stay-at-home mom and worked hard to learn how to fit in at the country club. His parents eventually accepted me into the family. The people at the country club didn't really. I knew that, but they were civil enough. They pretended to accept me, and I pretended that I belonged there just as much as they did. It's not that I didn't feel worthy—well maybe there was a little bit of that—but it just wasn't my thing. *Lunching* and playing tennis with people that I knew were not really my friends was not how I wanted to spend my day, but I tried hard because it was important to Andrew. He made sure I had the right kind of clothes and the right kind of car. I had to fight him a few years ago to get that minivan. He wanted me to get a Lexus instead. He didn't think a van sent the right message about his family. Honestly, just throw practicality out the window and pay more money for something just so people know we have plenty of it. *Ridiculous.*"

I take another long pull from my beer and continue.

"I admit that I liked having all those nice things, but I did feel guilty sometimes carrying around a purse that would have paid for three months of the mortgage on my parent's farm. I was practically bipolar going between *having a purse like this is a stupid waste of money* and *I am worthy of owning a purse that costs this much.* I tried really hard to be the kind of wife Andrew wanted, but it wasn't enough. I guess after fifteen years, Andrew was done slumming, and he moved on to greener pastures. I regret marrying Andrew, but I never regretted getting pregnant, and I've never thought of Hayes as a mistake. He and Audrey are the most wonderful parts of my life."

Jackson smiles. "They're awesome kids."

"Many of my so-called *friends* dropped me as soon as Andrew left me. It was predictable, really. I gave the pool rats lots to gossip about last summer."

"What about your family? Are they supportive?"

"I was close with my dad when I was younger. He was proud of me for staying the course and going to college. Mom didn't see the point. She thought it was fine for my sister to give her a grandchild at sixteen. She didn't understand my choice to move away. They came to visit a couple times in the beginning and were here for the wedding, of course, but they never fit in. I don't blame them since I still don't fit in." A sigh escapes. "I was here working hard to do all the things I needed to do to make Andrew happy, and my parents were working their farm. We grew apart. They were in a car accident five years ago, and they both passed away."

"Emmy." Jackson's word is a whisper.

I shrug. "My friend, Hope, went with me to the funeral. Andrew said he *couldn't get away from work*. The kids barely knew my family at that point, so I thought it was best if I went without them. It was better that way. After being away for so long, my family wasn't exactly welcoming."

"Was Andrew's family any better to you after that?"

"My mother-in-law warmed to me as time went on. Of course, she seems to like Carson well enough. Carson's family is wealthy, too, and they're old family friends, so apparently it's a match made in heaven."

"Andrew pushed hard to get the divorce through quickly. I didn't mind that. I didn't want to be married to him anymore. He made sure that I didn't get much of anything in the divorce settlement. In my starry-eyed youth, I had readily signed the prenuptial agreement when it was presented to me, so in a way, it's my own fault."

"No part of this is your fault." Another shrug.

"My best friend, Hope, works as an associate

dean of the business school. She's been able to pull some strings to allow my previous credits to count. Otherwise, I would have had to start all over with school. She also gave me a part-time job. Andrew does pay alimony and child support, but it isn't enough to live on. I was allowed to keep the jewelry that Andrew gave me, and that's all that I have of real value. When we sell the house, I will get half of the profit, but until it's sold I have to make the mortgage payments, and that's expensive. I'm just barely hanging on. I want to give the kids this last summer in the only home they've ever known. Once I graduate in August, I'll put the house on the market and move us out of here. I've already looked at a couple of small townhouses nearby where they would go to the same schools."

"I don't know what to say."

"You don't have to say anything. I'm not even sure why I'm telling you all of this. I just need to make smart decisions. No more regrets."

I walk to the refrigerator and get two more beers. Usually I just nurse one beer for hours, but tonight is a multiple beer night. Well deserved, I'd say.

"Maybe we can have a fresh start together. Do you like San Diego?"

*Seriously?*

I'm frozen in my tracks. Jackson's eyes widen slightly, but he quickly recovers. Is he just messing with me, or is he really asking me to move with him all the way across the country?

"You can't be serious. We just met. I don't know anything about you."

"Emmy, there's something here. I know you feel it. It was fate that I followed you yesterday. You just have to let yourself believe it."

*Been there. Done that. Will not be so quick to trust again.*

"Even if I was allowed to move my children away from Williamsburg, I can't drag them all the way across the country for something that *might be* fate. I can't regret that, too. Hayes and Audrey need to be here with their friends. Their lives have been rattled enough. You have your life, and I have mine. Our paths have crossed, but that's it. You have to leave tomorrow."

"Emmy, we all have regrets." Jackson's eyes cast downward before bouncing back up to mine. "Why do you want me to leave? Why don't you even want to give this a chance?"

"Because I can't."

"That's not an answer."

His eyes become hard. I've barely known him for twenty-four hours. How can he be angry at me for not wanting to move my family across the country?

"You need to leave, Jackson. You just need to leave."

He stands and does just that.

\*\*\*

The sun is setting as I trudge slowly down the walkway towards his truck. I should be rushing out to him, but my feet don't want to move.

*Please don't pull away before I get there.*

I was rude to him. I didn't mean to be, but I was. My fingers curl around the handle of the passenger door and pull. I climb up into Jackson's truck, closing the door behind me. I never take my eyes off Jackson as I do these things, but he keeps his gaze straight ahead, refusing to look at me.

"I'm sorry. I really am."

He still doesn't look my way. I scoot closer toward him on the big bench seat.

"My children are all I have, and I haven't had room for anyone else. I'm not sure what to do. Maybe this kind of thing is easy for you. For all I know, you date all the time. You're a freewheeling bachelor who's leaving town any minute. You're only going to hurt us."

He turns to me sharply. "You haven't even given me a chance."

"I know it's not fair to you, but I don't know how to do this. I wasn't looking for anyone and now, on top of that, I was held at gunpoint, and there's the e-mail issue. I just can't handle it all."

"What e-mail issue?"

*Crap.* Jackson's going to be even more mad at me because I didn't tell him about it. Huge sigh. *Here we go.*

"It looks like someone may have hacked my e-mail account. There actually is a Mr. Lehman. The men who met me yesterday were not him. The two guys from yesterday, or someone working with them, hacked my account and sent an e-mail that looked like it was from me to the real Mr. Lehman asking him to postpone our meeting until this morning."

*Can he even follow that?* Jackson's jaw tightens, and his eyes harden until there's no softness left.

"Why didn't you tell me? When did you find this out? I spoke with Detective Marshall earlier today, and he didn't tell me about this."

"I found out late this afternoon just before I came home. I forgot about it after seeing you here and then Andrew's visit. I'm sorry. I didn't withhold it from you intentionally."

Jackson's face begins to soften; his eyes, too.

"One thing at a time." Jackson pauses as he turns his body towards mine on his bench seat. "Does anyone else know your e-mail password?"

I shake my head. "I don't think so, but you can go ahead and yell at me because it's simply the names of my children. I know that I shouldn't do that, but I always figured that no one would care to read my e-mail. It's boring."

"I think I've gotten on your case enough today."

*That's a relief.*

"You need to change it to make it more secure and stop whoever hacked your account from doing it again. You need to make your password secure by adding numbers or a special character."

"I know."

Deflated, I look down at my clasped hands in my lap. *I thought you weren't going to lecture me anymore.*

"E-mail the real Mr. Lehman, and tell him that I will meet him tomorrow to make the sale."

*Wow.*

"You would do that for me?"

"I can't let you do it again."

My mouth forms into a smile, which is quickly returned by Jackson. He reaches out and gently caresses my cheek with his strong fingers. *Even his fingers feel muscular.*

"Emmy, you are a wonderful mother. There's no denying that, but you deserve to be happy, too."

My face flushes. Thank goodness I'm in the dark.

What do I say in response to that? Talking suddenly feels overrated. Instead, I lean in for a kiss. It's not like the kiss we shared in the house, full of passion and wanting. This is a kiss of gentleness and understanding. Jackson's lips, earlier firm, commanding, and sure, are now soft and caring. I pull away from him and look into his eyes. I trust Jackson. He won't hurt us, not intentionally, anyway.

"I'll call you when I set up the meeting with Mr. Lehman."

*He'll be in town at least one more night.* My stomach squeezes.

Jackson leans toward me and kisses me on the

cheek. *The cheek*? Disappointment fills me, but what did I expect? Push him away as much as I did, and I guess I'm lucky to get that.

"Goodnight, Emmy."

"Goodnight."

## Chapter Nineteen

### Jackson

Normally, I would kick some ass for someone calling me this late, but it doesn't matter tonight. Sleep isn't going to come anytime soon. It's easier to talk on the phone than to toss and turn.

*Smitty*.

"Dude, where have you been? I've been calling you all day."

"Sorry, man. I keep my phone off when I'm sleeping. Just remembered to turn it on and found a shitload of calls from you. What's going on that's so important? Are you in some kind of trouble?"

"No. I thought you might be."

"Me? Why would you think that?"

I need to be careful what I say here. Smitty's given me no real reason to doubt him. *But my gut doesn't lie.*

"I came by your house earlier. Banged on the door for a while, and you didn't answer."

"I sleep like death. Nothing wakes me up."

Well, that's new. We were trained to sleep so lightly that any sound would wake us up.

"Your car wasn't in the driveway."

"My car is in the shop getting new brakes and rotors. Is there something that you'd like to tell me? What the hell is going on?"

*What the hell is going on?* Good question. My gut has never let me down before, but I've got nothing.

"Based on the text that I got from Marco, I expected you to be calling me about whatever trouble *you* got into yesterday. Marco said that you took down two armed men all by yourself. Of course, I've seen you do better than that." His breathy laugh comes through the phone, louder than it should. "You're retired now, old man. You don't need to find that kind of action anymore."

"When did you get a text from Marco?"

"Just now, when I turned on my phone." Smitty's annoyance is clear. "I had three texts from him and two from Jamison asking if I'd heard from you. Are you in trouble with the police? Do you need my help this time? Tell me what happened."

"I was walking to my car after our lunch yesterday and saw a woman being held at gunpoint."

*He doesn't need to know that I was following her.* "I stepped in and took out the assailants." Nothing from Smitty. It would be so much easier to gauge his reaction in person rather than on the telephone. "The woman that I saved was actually the one that we saw yesterday."

Still nothing. *How can Smitty have no reaction? Does his lack of reaction mean something?*

"Do you mean the woman you said had too much money and too much attitude?"

"Yeah, that's the one."

*Still no sign of distress from Smitty.* No change in his breathing pattern. No unusual sounds or gasps.

"I was wrong on both counts, by the way. She doesn't have much of either. Well, she might have a little attitude, but just enough to be fun."

*This is good.* Maybe I was wrong and Smitty isn't involved in the robbery. I'm just an overly sensitized prick who wrongly accuses his friends of crimes.

"I hear ya. What do the police say about it?"

"They questioned me, but I'm off the hook with them. They have the two guys in custody."

"You going to be in town much longer?"

"I think I'll be leaving in the morning."

"Too bad. It would have been nice to see you again. Candy would have loved to see you, too. Oh well. Safe travels."

"Later, and remember, you can't call me *old man*. You're right behind me."

Smitty disconnects with a laugh.

Maybe I retired just in time. My gut has always been spot on, but this time I've accused a friend of a crime. What the hell is wrong with me?

***

*I'm leaving in the morning.*

The words caused instant heartburn that still won't go away. But why should they? Smitty is on the up-and-up. Maybe because I know that I went too far with her. Kissing Emmy was not in my plan. *Not that I hadn't thought about it.*

Am I kidding myself here? Did I really need to go back to check on Emmy today, or was it just because I wanted to see her again? Not sure I can answer that question. My motives couldn't have been completely unselfish if I asked her to move to California with me.

*What the hell was that?*

I give up on trying to rest and find a late-night bar in walking distance. This is not a night to get hammered, but maybe a couple beers will help me relax enough to nod off. The mugginess of the day is all but non-existent. There's even a light breeze, which is a nice change from the sweltering heat that we had here today.

Emmy didn't *really* want me to leave. I know that. She's scared. Shit, I'm scared. I never expected to fall for her. Sure, she's nice to look at, but the energy that zinged through my body when her lips touched mine was unprecedented. I haven't felt this hopeful about someone new since Katherine, and that sure as hell didn't end well. Emmy's experience with love hasn't been so great either, but then Andrew is an asshole. I was the asshole in my relationship with Katherine.

Emmy says she can't move away from Williamsburg. I can hardly believe I asked her to come with me. It's no wonder she wanted me to leave. I probably scared the shit out of her. The words just came blurting out of my mouth, and I know I looked just as surprised as Emmy did. And, although I meant it when I asked her to come with me, I'm the last thing that Emmy and her children need. I had my chance at a family, and I blew it. I know all too well that long distance doesn't work, and California is a hell of a long way from Virginia. Trying to make something out of this would be damn near impossible.

*But there's something about her.*

I take another long pull from my beer and set it down slowly on the bar. The place is practically empty, but being here isn't much better than my hotel room. Sitting around a bar with a couple of other dudes, trying to drink her away. *Not happening.* I've known Emmy barely twenty-four hours, and she has me practically crawling out of my skin. That kiss we shared—*stop thinking about it.* I've thought of kissing those lips almost constantly since I met her. Yet, somehow that kiss was even better than I had imagined it would be. Emmy's lips are as soft as I thought they would be, but when she kissed me back...*fuck, I have it bad.*

But, she asked me to leave. And not just leave her house—she asked me to leave town. *Not a good sign.* I bought more time by offering to meet Mr. Lehman for her. What happens after that? Do I get on the highway and just drive west like I was supposed to yesterday?

*I don't think I can.*

## Chapter Twenty

### Emmy

*I was right to tell Jackson to leave.* The words repeat over and over in my head, my mantra of sanity. If that's true, then why am I awake at three o'clock in the morning thinking about him? Thinking about that kiss. *Wow, what a kiss.* Sure I was nervous, and I scared him away, but there were other feelings, too. Feelings that I haven't felt in a very long time.

*So, so long.*

The kids are not happy that Jackson is gone. I told them yesterday that he wouldn't be in town for long, but that didn't stop their whining. Audrey tiptoed down the stairs earlier and peeked into the kitchen like she might interrupt something. All she found was me sitting at the kitchen table, feigning study. If I *had* been in a lip lock with Jackson at the time, we never would have heard her coming.

Hayes came in the door a few minutes later, excited to talk with Jackson about his workout. He stopped in his tracks when he saw me sitting alone. Hayes's handsome face fell. He's the spitting image of Andrew, except without the wealthy air and bitterness—all good things. Andrew always looks too serious. Hayes normally looks easy-going, but not tonight. He opened his mouth to say something, but must have decided against it because he turned and ran up the back stairs.

*Thunk.*

What was that? The noise isn't loud, but it isn't one of the usual sounds of our home either. My ears feel super-sensitive as I strain to hear anything that I can.

Is someone walking up the stairs? My thoughts immediately go to Hayes and Audrey. They were peacefully asleep when I checked on them earlier tonight. They haven't gotten out of bed.

All the doors were locked tonight. Jackson startled me enough with his appearance that I made sure everything was locked up tight before going to bed. It can't be Jackson. My body heats momentarily at the thought of him sneaking in for a booty call.

*Nope. No way.* Jackson wouldn't break into the house in the middle of the night to teach me a lesson. It freaked me out a bit to find him waiting in the driveway, but he was in the driveway. He didn't come into the house. The door was unlocked. He could have easily.

Is it Andrew? I've never known him to come over in the middle of the night, but would he do that? Is he trying to check up on me? Maybe he's trying to make a point since I yelled at him earlier?

*It has to be Andrew.* No one else has a key except for Anne, and there's no way she'd use it without permission. Maybe he's trying to catch me in bed with Jackson? Definitely something he would do. Like him catching me in bed with Jackson compares at all to me catching him in bed with Carson on our wedding anniversary. *Not even close!*

The footsteps stop in the doorway of my bedroom.

*Be still.*

*Don't even breathe.*

It's not like I can right now.

Too bad I'm not facing the door. Instead, I'm staring at the far wall, the exact opposite of where Andrew stands. He moves into the room ever so quietly, but my super-sonic hearing keeps pace with his steps. He stops at the dresser. Anger fills me from head to toe, replacing the fear. It pisses me off that Andrew would come here at night like this.

*I'll show him.* I bolt upright and shout, "What the hell are you doing?" I want to scare Andrew as much as he has scared me.

The man freezes, staring straight at me.

It's *not* Andrew.

It's *not* Jackson.

His dark outline is too short to be either man. For a frozen moment, we just stare at each other in the darkness. My good sense catches up with me, and I scream. The figure turns and bolts out of the room. I stumble clumsily off the bed and run into the hallway. Hayes's bedroom door flies open as my fingers find the switch for the hall light.

"Mom? What's wrong?"

"There was...someone...in my bedroom." My knees weaken, and I back into the wall behind me for support.

"Who was it?"

I shake my head. *Keep it together.* Do not break down in front of Hayes and now Audrey, who has joined us.

"I don't know."

Hayes sprints down the stairs after the intruder.

"No!"

Please let the man have a good head start. *Please don't let Hayes catch up to him.*

Audrey's arms move around my waist. I pull her closer to me, and we creep down the back stairs together. The kitchen door is wide open. It could have been left that way by the intruder or by Hayes or both.

My shaky fingers manage to dial 9-1-1 on the second try. I hold Audrey to me as I speak to the operator in choppy sentences. After a few deep breaths, my voice calms, and I'm able to explain what happened. The woman's voice is reassuring. She promises to send a squad car. I decline her offer to stay on the phone with me until they arrive.

Hayes comes in through the back door, out of breath, and joins our hug. We stand together in the kitchen until the police arrive.

*Thank you, God, for letting the intruder get away.*

## Chapter Twenty-One

### Jackson

"Mr. Jackson?" The voice is quiet and definitely young.

"Audrey? Is that you?"

"Yes."

*Shit. Something's wrong.*

"Are you okay?"

My feet hit the floor as I reach for my shorts in the darkness. I'm not sure what's going on over there, but I know I'll be heading to their house now, whatever the reason for her call. Thank goodness I didn't tie one on at the bar.

Audrey speaks softly, her voice measured. "We are okay, but can you come over?"

"What happened?" I still, my shorts half on, waiting for her answer.

"There was a man here. He's gone now, but..."

"Did you call the police?"

"Yes. They're talking with Mom now."

"I'll be there in five minutes."

I disconnect, grab a t-shirt and my keys, and hit the hallway at a run.

***

The guard lets me in after I give him my name. *Thank you, Audrey.* I don't want to lose any time dealing with a rent-a-cop right now.

Does Emmy even know that I'm coming? Does she know that Audrey called me? It doesn't matter. I would have come anyway as soon as I heard.

I slide my truck in behind one of the two police cruisers parked on the street. The cars are dark and silent, probably due to the time of night. The house is the opposite—lights blaze from every window.

The front door is slightly ajar. I jog up the front walk and push the door open enough for me to get through. Voices are coming from the back of the house. I walk towards them and find a group standing in the kitchen. My eyes lock with Emmy's immediately. Hers widen with surprise. *She didn't know that Audrey called me.*

"Jackson."

The group turns towards me. Hayes smiles.

Emmy doesn't, but she doesn't look upset either. Her chest rises with a deep breath. My own breath catches. It's all I can do not to run to Emmy and pull her into the safety of my arms. I'm here solely because I care about this woman. *How did this happen?*

"I called him, Mommy." Audrey speaks quietly, looking to her mother for approval. "His number was programmed in your cell phone."

Her arm slides around Audrey's shoulders. I walk closer to them, keeping my eyes on Emmy's. I stop short of hugging her to me. I want to—so badly, but I don't know how it would be received right now and in front of her children. *Shoot.* I don't know how she'd take it if it were just the two of us. The last time I saw her, she asked me to leave.

I introduce myself to the officers. There are four in the room. Three men, varying in age from mid-twenties to late forties, and a young woman obviously new to the force.

Emmy's eyes find mine again and a silent communication passes between us.

"So, Hayes? Audrey? Why don't we go in the other room and let your mom talk to the police? Hayes, I'd love to see your swimming trophies. I bet you have a ton."

Hayes and Audrey immediately look to their mom. Emmy smiles. It isn't very convincing, but she's trying.

"That sounds like a good idea. Why don't you do

that?"

I plaster a smile on my face as well and pat Hayes on the shoulder.

"Lead the way."

I'm not sure I've ever been in a house that is so large that it has more than one staircase. Emmy's house is pretty ostentatious, but even so, it somehow feels homey. No one would ever believe that she has money problems, living in a house like this.

What a flash from the past and my own teenage bedroom. Sure, Hayes's room is about three times as large as the cracker box that I had, and he has his own bathroom, but the decor of smelly socks and clothes covering the floor looks the same. I have to cut him some slack on the unmade bed, since it is the middle of the night, but by the looks of things, it doesn't get made much, even during the day. Apparently teenage boy filth transcends levels of socioeconomic status.

"*Wow.*"

The number of trophies and ribbons is impressive. Hayes's trophies are crowded together and still manage to take up an entire bookshelf and the top of his dresser. Hayes smiles proudly, but his smile doesn't reach his eyes. His gaze moves toward the door. I make a few comments about some of the larger trophies, and Hayes answers politely, but his mind is obviously preoccupied with his mother and the policemen downstairs.

"What about you, Audrey? Can I see your room?"

"I don't have as many trophies as Hayes."

She averts her eyes from mine, taking in the floor instead.

"Hayes is three years older than you. I'm sure you'll catch up."

That gets a smile from her, which I return and then follow Audrey down the hallway and into her bedroom. There's nothing about Audrey's room that reminds me of my own childhood. Plus, I do not have a sister, only a brother. This is totally uncharted territory. Her bed is large, white, and iron. A curtain of netting flows down from the ceiling and is tied at the corners of her bed. The colors are striking. The molding and chair rail are a bright white. A stark black is painted underneath the chair rail and a hot pink color above. A crazy color combination, yet it goes perfectly with Audrey's pink and black zebra print bedspread. *This is way out of my league.*

"Geez Audrey. The way you talked, I wasn't expecting much. You're going to catch up with Hayes in no time."

She has a very pretty smile to go along with her pink cheeks. *She looks so much like Emmy with that blush.*

"Most of mine are from soccer, though. I'm not so great at swimming."

"It's good to be diverse." She smiles again.

"She plays volleyball, too," Hayes adds, draping his arm across her shoulder. Such a sweet gesture.

My brother and I spent a lot of time beating the crap out of each other. That was our way of showing affection.

"You guys are really amazing." Hayes blushes a little. "Is there somewhere we can hang out and maybe watch some television? We need to stay out of the way while your mom finishes up?"

"Our TV room down the hall."

Audrey and I follow him farther down the hall past another bedroom, or maybe two, and then past the main staircase at the front of the house. Hayes hits the lights revealing a large room with a fireplace, overstuffed brown leather sectional sofa, and a huge television. He plops down, taking up one section of the couch, and powers on the TV. Audrey sits next to him, and I sit on the other end as Hayes channel surfs through the sludge of middle-of-the night programming. He settles on a Comedy Central movie. I don't care what we watch. My mind is on what's happening downstairs.

"Is our mom going to be okay?"

I look up to see Audrey's brown eyes on me. They're Emmy's eyes, for sure. Is this what Emmy looked like as a little girl? Hair braided down her back and everything? Hayes looks up, too.

"Your mom is a very strong woman. She's going to be just fine. Thank you for calling me, Audrey. I'm really glad that you did."

The corners of Audrey's mouth tip upward into the slightest of smiles.

"I'm glad you're here," Hayes adds. "Mom is, too. I could tell."

"Tell me what happened."

"Mom said that she was in bed but awake. She heard a noise downstairs. Then she heard someone come up the stairs and into her bedroom." My fingers are fisted tightly, my knuckles white. I release them and shake my fingers as Hayes continues. "Mom thought that it was Dad. She sat up and yelled at him, but as soon as she did, she realized that it wasn't him."

*Does Andrew often visit in the middle of the night?*

"Does she know who it was? What did he look like?"

Visions of Emmy being held at gunpoint the other day come to mind. This has to be related. It's too much of a coincidence.

"It was too dark for her to get a good look at him. He was standing near her dresser. Mom screamed, and he ran. I woke up when I heard her yelling and ran out of my room. She was in the hallway then. I ran after the guy, but I wasn't fast enough. I never even saw him."

"You ran after the intruder? Hayes, that's so dangerous."

"He scared my mom. He was in our house."

"I know he did. You were very brave to chase him but don't tell your mom I said that."

Hayes smiles. Audrey lets out a small giggle.

"What's going on in here?"

Emmy steps into the room. Dark lines encircle her lower eyelashes. She's wearing a pale purple tank top and matching floral pajama pants. She brushes a few strands of hair behind her ear.

"Is everything okay, Mom?" Audrey asks, but we all want to know.

"Yes, sweetheart. The policemen are checking for fingerprints on my dresser. I need to make sure that nothing is missing, but so far everything seems in place. He wasn't in my bedroom long enough to take anything."

"We're just fine in here. Don't worry about us."

Emmy gives me an appreciative look.

"I'll be back in a few minutes."

She turns and heads back down the hallway.

## Chapter Twenty-Two

### Emmy

It's surreal. Policemen move around my bedroom.

*There was someone in my house.*

It wasn't Andrew, and it wasn't Jackson. I stand in the corner of my bedroom and try to stay out of the way. The policewoman, Mary, retrieves a sweater for me from my closet as I rub my hands up and down my arms to stave off the chill. My brain knows that the cold feeling is from nerves and not actually the temperature of the air, but that realization doesn't make the goose bumps go away.

The break-in has to be related to what happened the other day, but the men who held me at gunpoint are still in jail. Is that what this man tonight was after? The bracelet? Why would someone go to all this trouble for my bracelet? It's valuable, but not worth all this effort.

It's easy to assume that he walked into the neighborhood, but I doubt he walked in at the gate. There's probably a camera there. He was probably smart enough to climb over the fence. It's decorative more than functional. It wouldn't be hard to do, but I never thought about that kind of thing until Jackson made me face it.

*Thank you, Audrey, for calling Jackson.*

I never would have called him, but I'm so relieved that he's here. The kids have heard enough. They don't need to relive the nightmare over and over again, each time I have to repeat the story to the police. I just wish I'd gotten a better look at the guy. I should have turned on the light. Guess there wasn't time for that though.

It's so frustrating to know so little. The only thing that's clear is that there is no sign of forced entry. The doors and windows were locked when we went to bed. *I'm positive.* The policemen say that there are no marks to show that the locks were picked. The most likely conclusion is that the intruder had a key. *A key to our house.* My already queasy stomach squeezes tighter. I will be calling a locksmith first thing in the morning. That's more money that I don't have and don't need to spend, but I'm going to change the locks, no question. I just can't afford it.

It's likely that the intruder wore gloves as well.

The police dusted the doorknobs, but they don't feel very confident about pulling a print that matters.

I fill them in on what happened the other day, and they promise to coordinate with Detectives Patterson and Marshall, who will be on duty in a couple hours.

It's almost five o'clock by the time they depart, leaving only twenty minutes until my alarm is due to sound. I send a quick text to Hope and explain that I won't be at work today. The money is important, but the thought of leaving home makes my eye twitch. I'm a mess.

I drag myself back up the stairs to check on my family. Jackson is watching *Stripes* at a very low volume. Hayes and Audrey are both sound asleep on the couch.

Jackson stands, tucks a blanket around Audrey, and walks towards me. I walk a few steps back into the hallway, and that's where Jackson meets me. Without a word, he pulls me into his arms. *I let him*.

I want to be lost in his strong arms.

I want to be warm.

I want to be safe.

Jackson gives me all these things and just lets me *be*. He doesn't ask questions. He just holds me. He's here with me.

"Thank you." The words are practically choked out in a mixture of whisper and sob. "Thank you for being here."

I pull back and look into his eyes, eyes that are

soft and caring.

"I don't want to be anywhere else."

Jackson doesn't make a move of any kind. He just continues to hold me. He likely doesn't want to take advantage of me when I'm the damsel in distress, but I don't want to be the damsel. *I want him to kiss me.* As if picking up on my unspoken wish, Jackson's hand caresses my jawline ever so lightly. He tips my chin up. His lips move to mine, tenderly grazing. Electricity passes between us. Then the small amount of space between our bodies is no more as his mouth takes mine completely. I'm fantastically trapped between Jackson's hard body and the wall behind me.

My body is a mass of dizzying sensations. My arms move to his shoulders and then to the base of his neck. His tongue moves in my mouth in wonderful exploration.

Jackson pulls away suddenly, leaving me breathless. A smile creeps across his face, a smile that I can't help but return. He takes my hand in his and pulls me down the stairs to the living room.

"Let's talk about what happened. Can I get you anything first?"

How sweet is it that he's offering me something to drink in my home? It's nice to be taken care of, but it's strange.

"I'm okay. Just sit with me."

Jackson does sit, close to me. He takes my hand again in his, lightly tracing my fingers with the index finger of his other hand.

"Did you get a good look at him?"

I shake my head. Tears are close.

Did he take anything?"

Another shake.

"No, nothing. They are pretty sure that he wore gloves and that he used a key to get in the kitchen door from the deck."

Jackson's body stiffens. "Who has a key to that door?"

"I didn't know that anyone did. I don't even have a key to the back door, that I know of anyway. We enter through the front door, with a key, or through the garage, using the keypad for the automatic door opener. I heard the intruder come up the back stairs from the kitchen, and he did exit that way, so they assume that's the way he came in. Hayes says that the back door was wide open when he ran downstairs to chase the guy."

"And you're sure that all the doors were locked?"

"I'm positive."

A shiver moves up my spine. His arm moves around my shoulders. I feel his warmth instantly.

"I'll replace the locks today. We should get a quote for an alarm system, too."

"No, I don't want an alarm system. They cost too much money."

Jackson already knows about my money issues, so I can tell him the truth.

"They have ads on television all the time when

companies run specials, or I could install one myself."

"You've done so much already. Besides, my kids and their friends are in and out of the house constantly. Our neighbors always have problems with their alarms getting set off accidentally, usually by cleaning people or someone else working on the house. The police come a couple times at no charge, but after a few of those mistaken visits, the prices for the police go way up. I definitely can't afford that."

"Emmy, I want to help you."

Jackson speaks with such sincerity that his words bring tears to my eyes.

"How about just the locks, and I pay for them?" Jackson's mouth is set in a determined line, but he stops arguing. "I appreciate everything you've done. I really do. I've already delayed you a couple days. You should be in Oklahoma by now. You weren't even supposed to stay one night in Williamsburg."

My eyes fill completely with tears.

"And I was so rude to you earlier. I didn't really want you to leave."

"I know."

His tone is slightly mischievous, but he doesn't try to kiss me. Instead he presses my head down onto his shoulder. The longer Jackson stays, the harder it's going to be to let him go.

## *Chapter Twenty-Three*

### *Jackson*

*I am in so much trouble.*

Emmy is so close, her head rests on my shoulder. Every breath I take brings more of her into me. Her scent—something floral. What does a gardenia smell like?

*Look what she's doing to me.*

She has me thinking of things I shouldn't be thinking about—gardenias and what it would be like to hold Emmy every night. Would every kiss we share be as amazing as our first? Probably not, but if it's even half as good...

*I am in so much trouble.*

## Chapter Twenty-Four

### Emmy

I awaken with a start. I'd been dreaming that there was a man in my house—and there is. It's just that the man is Jackson and not the faceless, dark outline of a stranger who violated my bedroom.

My brain finally catches up with the reality that Jackson is waking me. A kind of numbness spreads through me as if I awoke in the wrong phase of sleep or something. I was *really* out. I bring my hand to my mouth and do a quick check for drool. *None, thank goodness.* I smile with relief. Jackson returns my smile with the biggest one I've seen on him. His teeth are white against his tan skin. His whole face brightens, his blue eyes somehow illuminated from within.

*Thank goodness* I'm sitting because I think my legs just melted. He tucks a piece of hair behind my ear.

"I'm really sorry to wake you, but someone is here."

I jump up and run to the window in time to see my mother-in-law—make that *ex-mother-in-law* exit her Mercedes.

*So much for my good mood at waking up in Jackson's arms.*

Vanessa looks right and left, down both sides of the street, and then studies our house. It isn't surprising to see her, but I am surprised that's she's here at 8:17 in the morning. I pull my sweater tighter around me to ward off another chill.

"Is that Andrew's mother?" Jackson has walked up behind me. "Do you want me to go upstairs?"

"No way."

"I just don't want to make things worse for you."

I grab for Jackson's hand. His fingers entwine with mine.

"Never. She is a bit...intense, but her heart is in the right place."

"Why don't I make some coffee?"

"That would be great."

He turns and heads toward the kitchen. I pull the door open before Vanessa rings the bell. No reason for her visit to wake Hayes and Audrey. I'm letting them sleep through swim practice. They won't be happy with me, but they need their rest after last night's drama.

"Emmy," Vanessa squeaks in a high-pitched whine. "I came as soon as I heard. You poor dear."

She grabs me for a hug and kiss. It's not a hug full of feeling. Instead, it's more of a *technical* kind of hug. Her arms go around me, and therefore, it fulfills the definition of a hug without the warmth that's supposed to be the point of a hug in the first place. She makes a kiss noise next to my cheek without actually kissing it. I'm not sure what the point is of that either. It's not just me. This is how she usually greets Andrew and her grandchildren. She's not the warm, huggable kind of grandma.

"Come on in, Vanessa."

Maybe if I speak quietly, she'll get the hint to pipe down and not wake up the kids. I can exist on no sleep and coffee, but they aren't as good at pulling it off and need as much sleep as they can manage.

She sashays inside, and I close the door behind her. Her eyes travel down to my bare feet and then back up to my face. My rumpled pajamas and disheveled hair are quite a contrast to her petal pink sheath with black trim and matching pumps. Her make-up is perfectly fresh. Her hair is perfectly styled. I clear my throat involuntarily and hug my sweater more tightly to me.

"It was a late night. I just woke up."

Was that really the best choice of words with a man in the kitchen? *Whatever.* If Vanessa gets the wrong idea, then she does. It doesn't matter. She's not my mother-in-law anymore.

Jackson appears in the doorway then and walks towards us. Vanessa clears her throat in a grand gesture, as if she just walked in on us while we were making out. She's always been a bit over-dramatic. That's definitely where Andrew gets it from.

"Vanessa, this is Jackson. Jackson, this is Vanessa, Andrew's mother."

They shake hands but eye each other skeptically.

"So wonderful to meet you, Jackson. You must be the gentleman who was with Emmy at the swim meet the other day." Jackson's eyes widen slightly, leaking a little bit of surprise that she has heard about him. "This town isn't that big. I hear a lot of things, especially when they have to do with my Emmy."

*My Emmy.*

She's been calling me that for a while now. It was strange the first time, but it's her way of showing me that she hasn't given up on me, even with Carson around. She hasn't come through with any financial support, but I wouldn't take money from her anyway. Still, I appreciate her effort—for the kids' sakes, especially—and I'm trying to be a forgiving person. It would likely help if she were warmer and more loving as a person, but she just isn't. This is about as warm as she gets.

Jackson holds his own against her gaze. I'm sure he's used to women checking him out, but Vanessa isn't like *normal* women. Her eyes feel like an x-ray —no, more than an x-ray—like she can see into your soul.

"How did you hear about the break-in?"

"Oh, my Andrew called me as soon as he got to the courthouse and heard the news. I rushed right over to see if there's anything that I can do. Is everyone okay? Did they take anything?"

"We are fine, at least physically. Hayes chased him away."

Her hands fly to her now open mouth.

"Oh, dear! My poor Hayes! I've just been worried sick since Andrew told me about this."

A big sigh involuntarily releases. This is a lot of drama to handle with only a couple hours of sleep.

"May I speak with you alone for a moment?" she asks, with a look in Jackson's direction.

He takes a step backwards.

"I'll go check on Hayes and Audrey."

Jackson looks at me quickly for permission. When I don't decline his offer, he turns and moves up the stairs.

"Would you like to sit down?"

I follow her over to the living room and take a seat next to her on the couch. The spot is still warm from where I was sleeping only moments ago.

"I am so relieved that you and the children were unharmed last night. I really am." Vanessa's eyes show her sincerity, and I feel myself relax. I'm not sure how to respond to that, so I say nothing. She continues. "I know that you're probably happy to have this big, strong man around with everything that's been happening." *Crap. Does that mean she knows about the jewelry problem, too? Andrew II does have a way of knowing too much.* "Please exercise caution with this man, Emmy. How long have you known him? Do you really know anything about him?"

She looks at me expectantly, and I realize that she actually wants an answer. I thought that these were questions she wanted me to ponder on my own.

"I've known Jackson a couple days."

"A couple days?" The surprise is evident in her expression. "You've known him for such a short amount of time, and you're already allowing him into your home?"

I don't miss her real meaning. She thinks I'm sleeping with him. Can't really blame her for that though, since she did find us together this morning. It pisses me off. She has no right to lecture me after what her son did in our home when we were still married. *Not that Andrew's actions were her fault, but still.*

"What I do in my own home is *none* of your business."

"I completely understand that, Emmy. I'm not judging you. I just want you to be careful. Maybe it isn't a coincidence that all of this started around the same time that you met Jackson."

*This conversation is over.* I stand and face her.

"I appreciate your *concern*, but I met Jackson when he saved me from being robbed."

Vanessa stands, too.

"Please be careful, Emmy. I only meant to help."

With the last word, *because she always has to have the last word*, Vanessa turns, opens the door, and walks out.

## Chapter Twenty-Five

## *Jackson*

"How do you put up with these people?"

I move closer and place Emmy's warm hand between both of mine.

"As you can see, I'm not very good at it. Vanessa means well, and I'm pretty sure that I overreacted."

"No way. I think your patience is remarkable."

"My relationship with Vanessa started out pretty rough, but she's been making an effort the last few years. She started really trying before Carson even moved back to the area. I'm not sure what really changed. Maybe she just gave up and realized that I wasn't going anywhere. Then, when Carson came into the picture and Vanessa could be done with me, she began trying even harder." Emmy sighs heavily. "I don't know. Part of me is done with her, but she is the grandmother of my children, and she's trying. I feel like I should do my best to let her."

"Let's get some coffee."

I link her fingers with mine and pull her towards the kitchen. When we arrive at her coffee pot, I find myself not wanting to let go of her hand. A sigh escapes at the realization that this little quandary mirrors our bigger situation. I don't want to leave. I don't want to let go of Emmy, but she won't let me stay.

I turn her around slowly and hug her to me. Her arms circle my neck and she rests her head against my chest. She squeezes me tightly, holding me as if she doesn't want to let go either. Feeling Emmy's body against mine brings out all kinds of thoughts that I have to school. She's been through too much, not to mention that her children are upstairs. With a lot of restraint, I pull myself away and guide her to a seat at the head of the kitchen table. I return and place a mug of hot coffee on the table in front of her.

"What kind of work does Andrew's father do at the courthouse?"

"He's a judge, and a pretty high-powered one, too —locally anyway. He knows everything that happens in this town. It was clear from what Vanessa said that they know about me selling my jewelry. I really wish they didn't. I don't want anyone to know about that."

I place a hand on hers. "Don't worry about it. You have to do what you have to do."

"I know, but it's embarrassing. Plus, I don't want her to worry that I might try to sell the Rutledge ring."

"The what?"

"Back in the early days, when Andrew was in love with me, he gave me a family heirloom—a Rutledge ring. Mr. Rutledge was a renowned jewelry designer back in the 1800's. The ring is worth a lot of money, and more than that, it's been in their family for more than one hundred years. It belonged to his great-grandmother. It's really beautiful. It has an emerald cut diamond surrounded by small diamonds."

"It sounds like it's yours to sell if you want to."

Emmy shrugs. "It is, and it isn't. It was part of the divorce settlement that if I ever want to sell it, I have to get it appraised and then offer the sale to Andrew's family first at the appraisal price. If they decline the offer of sale, then I can sell it however I would like for the appraisal price, but no lower. I don't ever plan to sell it though. Well, I would if I needed the money to prevent us from starving, but I would never sell it to some random guy like my other jewelry. It's worth far more than that." Emmy's fingers trace the handle of her coffee mug. "Maybe I should let myself sell it. I don't want the stupid thing, but I *really* don't want *Carson* to get it."

She sighs a huge sigh.

"What?"

"I was elated when Andrew gave me that ring. We were getting married, and I was in love with him. His parents were so angry that Andrew gave me the Rutledge ring. That's how it was supposed to work in their family. The oldest son gives it to his wife and so on. That gesture was so important to me at the time, but it sure doesn't mean crap now." Her gaze meets mine. "And I shouldn't be talking about any of this with you. I'm sorry."

"Don't be."

Andrew is such an ass. Emmy was clearly devastated when he left her. And why would he? She's perfect.

"Why don't I email Mr. Lehman from my account and see if I can meet him this afternoon? Anytime is fine."

"Thank you for meeting him." She takes a breath and tucks a stray piece of hair behind her ear. She's taking time to prepare herself for something. "Listen, the kids will be with Andrew tonight. Will you stay in town one more night if I make you dinner—as a thank you for all you've done for us?"

"Why don't we go out instead?" Her mouth opens in protest, but I continue. "I'm sure dinner here would be wonderful, but if I'm going to be in Williamsburg, then I want to go to one of those taverns where the servers wear costumes."

"Seriously? Those are tourist traps. I'm a great cook."

I shrug instead of responding with words. I don't know what to say. Truthfully, I don't want Emmy to go through the effort for me. I want to take care of her.

"Seriously. I'm sure you're a phenomenal cook, but let's go out."

"Okay. I guess."

Guilt fills me. For what, I'm not quite sure.

I stand and kiss her quickly on the cheek. I feel like I just lied and need to make a break for it.

"I'm running out to the hardware store. Please lock up while I'm gone, and don't let anyone in other than the police."

# Chapter Twenty-Six

## Emmy

*Great.*

Jackson all but ran away from me just now. Am I pushing things with him? Did he take my dinner invitation as an offer of more than dinner? And if he did, then why is he insisting we have dinner out? Is that his way of telling me that nothing more will come of this than a couple hot kisses? That sure isn't what it feels like when Jackson kisses me. It feels like it's all he can do to hold onto his control.

Still, there is something between us that's more than attraction. The realization makes me smile even if it does scare the crap out of me. It's more of a shock to me than anyone. *I mean come on, this was not in my plan.* I've been asked out on multiple occasions, and I turned them all down. My plan is to concentrate solely on my children. Get my degree. Move to our own place. Do the best that I can for them. Somehow Jackson blew through all my defenses. Sure, I don't know much about him, but I'd really like to find out.

Two short raps at the door make me jump. *I am way too tense.*

I look around the corner into the hallway and make out the figure peeking in through the glass window panes that line the sides of the front door.

Anne stands there in a sweat suit and flip flops, her short blond bob shimmering in the morning sunshine.

Jackson said not to let anyone in, but his rules don't apply to Anne.

I unlock the door to her smiling face.

"Well?"

"Well, what?"

"Well, how was it? He is soooo hot. You go girl." Her light blue eyes twinkle. I step back just in time to avoid a collision as she barrels through the doorway.

"That hasn't happened."

*Yet, I hope.*

"Yeah. Right. The kids. But there's always tonight, right? Wednesday night. Andrew's night to take them. Huh?" Is she reading my mind, or am I that transparent? She pulls me to her in a tight hug. "Give me a break already. Go. For. It."

She pushes past me and saunters towards the back of the house. I lock the door—I'm careful to do that now—and join her in the kitchen as she's pouring herself a cup of coffee.

"I swear I almost peed my pants when I looked outside and saw his truck in the driveway...again. I sent the kids to swim practice on their bikes this morning because I couldn't stand not talking to you about it one more second. It was a toss-up though. I bet the gossip mongers are freaking out."

Anne looks at me expectantly, ready for something juicy.

"Speaking of gossip mongers."

A playful smile forms on my lips. We giggle together.

"You know that I won't say anything. Now stop stalling, and spill it."

I spend the next hour filling Anne in on almost everything that's happened in the past few days. She knows that I've been planning to sell my jewelry, but she didn't know that I'd started already. I don't tell her about being held at gunpoint or meeting with strangers in semi-deserted locations. I don't feel like a lecture right now, and I know that I don't have a good excuse. Desperation makes you do crazy things.

"I *loved* watching Marci flirt with Jackson at the pool the other night. She made such a fool of herself —not that that's anything new. Jackson was polite, but you could tell that Marci was starting to get on his nerves. Is it true that Jackson doesn't live here? That he's moving to California?"

"Yeah. He wasn't even supposed to stay here for a night."

"And he's still here. Wonder why that is?"

"He asked me to move to California with him." I say the words quietly, avoiding eye contact. Feels like a confession.

"He what?"

Anne's exclamation is way too loud in our quiet house. I shush her immediately, and we again giggle like teenagers.

"He did. I'm not even sure that he meant it. Or, if he did, maybe he's changed his mind. He just kind of blurted it out when we had dinner together last night. He couldn't have meant it, and besides, even if he did mean it, it doesn't matter. I'm not uprooting my children after all that they've been through. It's bad enough that I have to move them out of the only house they've ever known. I'm not moving them across the county. They're all I have left."

"Not true. You have a hot guy asking you to move away with him. *Not* that I want to get rid of you, but it does give you something to think about."

"Besides the fact that our divorce documents clearly forbid a move, this is my life. Real life. It's not a romance novel where I run away with Prince Charming—whom I just met, mind you—and everything turns out perfectly. I know very little about him."

I really do need to remedy that. Jackson knows way too much about me.

\*\*\*

Jackson's all smiles when I open the door for him, but his face tightens into a glare as soon as he sees Anne. He stops short as he steps into the kitchen, causing me to do the same to avoid running into the back of him. Anne laughs, her blue eyes twinkling.

"It's nice to see you again, Anne."

Jackson's words are polite, but his eyes are not. Anne's smile fades a little. He pulls two lock sets out of a bag and places them on the kitchen table.

"Guess that's my cue to leave." She stands and hugs me goodbye. I walk her to the door. "Jump him now. I don't know why he's pissed, but you could help him with that."

"*Anne!*"

My eyes widen with surprise. We share another laugh before I close and lock the door behind her.

Jackson leans against the arch that leads into the kitchen, his arms folded in front of him. His shirt sleeves strain against his flexed muscles. Steam is coming out of his ears. His eyes are intense.

"Why are you so angry?"

"Is Anne a policewoman?"

So that's it. Jackson did say not to let anyone

inside except for the police. This, however, is my house, and Anne is one of my best friends. Who is Jackson to tell me who I can let into my own home? My smile disappears completely as I walk towards him.

"You're not the boss of me."

I wish I were taller so that I could have impact. Of course, that might work better if I don't say things like *You're not the boss of me*. Very mature, Emmy. Where did that even come from? I walk past Jackson into the kitchen, pour myself a glass of water, and stand next to the sink as I sip it.

My vision focuses on the wall across the room, but I see Jackson walk towards me in my peripheral vision.

"Don't do that."

"Don't do what?"

*Drink water?* I know that's not what he means, but it's the first thing to come to my mind. The mind that I think I'm losing. Maybe I can't actually exist on three hours of sleep and coffee.

Jackson sighs heavily. His fingers cup my chin, warm and unyielding. He turns my face toward his. My gaze remains straight ahead. I refuse to look up at him and melt into his stupid blue eyes, which is exactly what I will do if I see them. Jackson steps directly in front of me. Now I'm forced to stare at his chest, which is tight against the cotton of his t-shirt. *Not helping*. What does his bare chest look like? It's no wonder SEALs are known for their muscles. If I could just see them without his stupid t-shirt in the way.

Jackson removes the water glass from my hand and places it on the counter next to me.

"Don't be so stubborn. I'm only concerned about your safety."

His voice is deep and caring. *What was I mad about?* Oh yeah, Jackson bossing me around.

"Anne is my friend. She isn't a threat."

He sighs heavily and pulls me to him. His breath mixes with my own as his lips move over mine. I'm a goner.

I surrender completely. Jackson's tongue dances with mine. My hands move over Jackson's muscular back. *Wow.* He lifts me up onto the countertop, and I pull him even closer to me. A groan escapes from his throat. My hands move over his sides and under his shirt to explore his chest. I skim each ripple of muscle, going weak with thoughts of kissing him there, allowing my tongue to lick his beautiful, chiseled chest as I travel downward. *Oh gosh.* This is going to happen. *Please let this happen.* I've never wanted anyone like this.

My legs circle his waist, and he's even closer, fitting just right where he should. I pinch the hem of his t-shirt between my fingers and tug upwards.

"Wait. Not here."

He steps backwards so that I'm no longer sitting on the countertop. His hands support my butt as he carries me towards the back stairs. *Please let me be wearing nice panties.*

The ring of the telephone echoes through the house. *Crap.* It would be easy to ignore a phone call right now except that the ringing will wake up my children, and this isn't just any ring. It's the special tone that indicates the front gate is calling. We have a visitor.

My legs drop to the floor. I hold onto Jackson's shoulders for a second to steady myself. He's breathing heavily, too, but he's smiling, and before I know it, so am I.

I dash for the phone and grab it during the middle of the fourth and last ring.

"Hello."

"Hi there, Emmy, honey. It's Carter."

The sound of his voice makes me smile. Years of smoking have given Carter a very distinct baritone voice, and I know that it's a security guard calling, but he always identifies himself. He's such a sweetie.

"Good morning, Carter. How are you this morning?"

"I'm okay. I just wanted to give you some warning. Two police detectives are here to see you. I went ahead and let them through, so they're on their way, but I wanted to give you a heads up anyway. Very sorry to hear about what happened last night. Is there anything that I can do for you?"

"We're okay. Thank you for letting me know."

"I mean that, sweetie. Anything I can do for you, I'm at your disposal."

"I know. Thanks, Carter."

"How did dinner go last night with your new Casanova?"

My eyes roll involuntarily, but a full smile breaks onto my face.

"Dinner was good."

I'm saved from any more discussion by the ringing of the doorbell. The chime echoes through the house. The kids are surely awake now.

"They're here. I have to run now. Thanks again."

"I'll get the details from you later, Missy."

With that, he hangs up.

## Chapter Twenty-Seven

### Jackson

Emmy answers the door when the bell rings, but it isn't the detectives standing on the steps. Instead, Andrew looks back at us. He's dressed the part of the business man: dark charcoal suit, silk tie, French cuffs. Emmy's spine stiffens as if preparing for battle. His eyes dart to me briefly, but Andrew turns his attention to Emmy. His eyes are soft, lacking the hardness they displayed yesterday.

"I heard about what happened. I'm so sorry, Emmy."

"Is that why you came here?" Emmy's tone is not as nice, but who can blame her?

Andrew nods. He spares another look in my

direction.

"Yes, and I would like to apologize for my behavior. I was a bit of a jerk when I was here last night. Can we start over? I'm Andrew Bennet, III."

He makes direct eye contact with me now as he holds his hand out to me. I shake it.

"Ed Jackson."

"Very nice to meet you."

Andrew doesn't smirk when he says it, although even with his apparent change of heart, I have a hard time believing that it's *nice* to meet me.

"Would you like a cup of coffee?"

Emmy's mouth opens in surprise. I know that I probably shouldn't be inviting people, especially Andrew, into her home for a beverage, but I want to study him a little bit. The detectives should get to meet him, if they haven't already. *What's taking them so long?*

Andrew looks at Emmy.

"Is that okay?"

"Sure." She doesn't look like it's okay, an obviously fake smile on her face. The three of us head to the kitchen. I gesture for Andrew and Emmy to sit at the table, and I pour the coffee.

"Changing the locks?"

Andrew lifts one of the lock packages and studies it carefully. It looks awkward in his hand. Andrew doesn't seem like the kind of guy who's very handy around the house.

"Yes. It looks like the intruder had a key, so I

want to make sure that it doesn't work anymore."

"Maybe you should get an alarm system, Emmy."

"*I can't afford an alarm system*."

Emmy's frustration comes through loud and clear. Hopefully she's more angry at Andrew over the fact that he doesn't give her enough money to live on and not frustrated from our earlier conversation. Andrew quickly places the lock package back on the table.

I'm just about to sit down with them when the doorbell rings. *The detectives*.

Emmy and I answer the door together leaving Andrew alone in the kitchen. Detective Patterson's eyes widen at the sight of me, but she shouldn't be surprised. My truck is parked in the driveway. We all shake hands, and then Emmy escorts us to the living room.

"I guess I'll be going for now."

We all look up to see Andrew standing awkwardly nearby. The detectives both study him curiously.

"Detective Marshall, Detective Patterson, this is my ex-husband, Andrew Bennett."

Detective Patterson's eyes widen further as she looks from Andrew to me. "Well isn't this cozy?"

Detective Marshall gives her a look that wipes the smirk off her face and makes her stop talking, but her eyes still look amused. Andrew nods towards the detectives and walks out the door.

\*\*\*

Emmy offers lemonade and coffee to the detectives, but neither takes her up on it. She sits next to me on the love seat. My hand finds hers, and our fingers intertwine. Emmy's hand is so tiny compared to mine, but the two still somehow fit together perfectly.

Agent Patterson's eyes roam around the room, taking in everything. She's very perceptive, which is probably one of the reasons she's made detective so young. She just needs to learn to keep her mouth closed, or maybe learn to say the opposite of whatever she's thinking. She pulls out her notebook again and begins the questioning.

"So, you two have become quite close in the last couple of days. You're still here huh, Mr. Jackson? I thought you'd be halfway to California by now."

Emmy winces at her words. *Great.*

"I have a month before I need to be in California. I'm in no hurry, and I'm enjoying my time here."

I give Emmy's hand a squeeze. She gives me a forced smile that doesn't reach her eyes. Detective Marshall watches Emmy as well.

"So, Ms. Bennett, you're sure that nothing was actually taken last night?"

Emmy sits a little straighter.

"Yes, I'm sure. They didn't get a chance. I thought that it might be my ex-husband, so I yelled at him and scared him away. My son took off after him, but he got away. Thank goodness he did. I mean, I want him caught, but I didn't want Hayes to be the one to catch him."

"I could have handled it, Mom."

We all turn and see Hayes walking into the room from the foyer. Emmy stands, walks to him, and gives him a tight hug.

"I know, but I'm your mom. I worry."

His expression softens. Placated, he turns and walks into the kitchen. Emmy returns and takes her seat next to me. She doesn't take my hand.

Detective Marshall continues, "We checked out the real Mr. Lehman. His story checks out. However, I'm sorry to say that after speaking with him, he has changed his mind about purchasing your bracelet. I think talking with the police scared him away. I'm sorry about that, Ms. Bennett."

Emmy doesn't speak, but her disappointment is evident.

"This house is huge. I'm sure you can find other things to sell."

Detective Patterson's words were probably meant to somehow cheer Emmy up, but they don't help. Again, this woman *really* needs to work on her people skills.

"Yeah. I'm sure I'll find something." Emmy sighs.

"Does your ex-husband make it a practice to come into your home in the middle of the night?"

Emmy shakes her head. A blush of anger begins working its way up her neck.

"He never has, but the doors were locked when we went to bed, and he's one of the two people who has a key."

"Who is the other?"

"My neighbor, Anne Shelly. She lives two doors down and keeps a spare key for me in case of emergency. I'm sure that the intruder wasn't Anne or her husband."

Detective Patterson takes more notes.

"So, have you made any progress on the investigation? Who were those men you arrested? How did they find out about my meeting with Mr. Lehman in the first place?"

Detective Patterson answers. "They are two-bit thieves who have both been arrested for petty theft in the past. Hacking your email isn't their typical style, they're usually more *grab and go* kind of thieves."

"Are they associated with anyone else? Maybe someone who could have broken in here last night to steal the bracelet?"

"The two of them work together as a team. They aren't known to work with anyone else."

"But the two incidents have to be connected." The frustration is clear in my words.

Agent Marshall turns his body towards me. "We think so, but we haven't yet found a link. We have nothing to go on for the robbery last night. No fingerprints. No forced entry. Nothing. You really should think about changing your locks, Ms.

Bennett."

"I'm planning to do that this afternoon."

"Good. Good." Agent Marshall stands. Agent Patterson follows his lead. "This is still a very active investigation. In the meantime, it's good that you have Mr. Jackson here to keep you company." He flashes me a knowing grin and then looks away quickly.

Emmy and I stand and follow the detectives to the door. "Thank you for your time. Please call me if there is anything else that happens, or you think of something that you've forgotten regarding this case."

I move to pull Emmy into my arms as soon as the door closes. She pushes me away just as Hayes rounds the corner.

"What else is going on, Mom? What was the thing they were saying about selling a bracelet?"

Emmy's eyes widen. Her mouth opens, but she closes it quickly and smiles. "Oh, it's nothing." She turns and begins walking toward the back of the house. "I have an old bracelet that I don't want anymore that I wanted to sell. I saw one of those commercials on television the other night about companies that will pay you for your gold. It just got me thinking. I don't wear the bracelet anymore, so I thought I might give it a try. That's all."

"Why were the police asking about it?"

"They ask about everything. Because of what happened last night, they checked out the buyer that I found on Craig's List. They did it just to be nice, but then, because the police were checking on it, the buyer bailed. It's not a big deal." Emmy flashes him a full smile that Hayes doesn't return. He's not believing her story. It's no wonder. She's doing a horrible job of lying. Hayes turns and studies me next. *Think blank expression*. This is between Emmy and Hayes. *Don't get involved*.

"I understand why you let me sleep through swim practice, but I'd like to go to the pool and swim some laps anyway. Is that okay with you, Mom?"

Emmy visibly relaxes at the change of subject.

"Sure, sweetie."

Hayes grabs a banana from the bunch on the countertop, kisses his mom on the cheek, and walks out the door that leads to the garage.

"You should tell him the truth."

I shouldn't get involved in this—it's between Emmy and her son—but the words came out anyway.

Emmy sighs. "I know, but I can't tell him everything. I have to protect Hayes and Audrey from this mess. They've been through enough."

I move to her and caress her cheek lightly. "You can't keep them in the dark forever you know."

"I know, but I'm going to protect them for as long as I can."

\*\*\*

The doorbell chimes...again. What is it with all

these visitors? At least Emmy has people who care about her. This time it's a repeat—Vanessa Bennett. She walks into the foyer as soon as Emmy opens the door.

"I just couldn't stop thinking about you this morning and how frightening it must have been to have a stranger sneaking through your home. So, I went to Harry's and got this lovely take-out lunch. There are sandwiches and his famous potato salad."

She lifts up the large white bag in her hand and continues to speak about pickles and special mustard in an overly-cheery tone as she walks toward the back of the house. Emmy and I follow silently and watch her as she places the bag on the countertop.

"Thanks so much, Vanessa. Would you join us?"

"No, no. I don't mean to get in the way."

*Yet you're always here.*

Emmy tilts her head and steps closer to Vanessa.

"Of course you wouldn't be in the way."

Vanessa smiles.

"I'm due to meet a friend for lunch at the club, but thank you for inviting me." Her smile fades. "I'm sorry that I left here on bad terms earlier. What you do in your home is none of my business. I sincerely apologize if I overstepped my bounds. You know I love you, Emmy." Emmy closes the gap between them and gives Vanessa a hug. "I'm glad to see that you have someone who can help you change the locks." She picks up one of the packages and looks at it distastefully.

"Andrew was never very handy in that way." Emmy and I share a smile. "I must be going now. Enjoy your lunch."

Emmy walks her to the door.

\*\*\*

The rest of the afternoon goes quickly. It helps that there are no more visitors, and I keep myself busy. I change the locks on Emmy's front and back doors. There are two sets of French doors that lead to the deck, but they don't have a key, so there's no point in changing those. I leave the new keys on Emmy's kitchen counter.

Audrey woke up around noon, ate some breakfast, and rode her bike to the pool to meet her friends. Emmy and I have been alone in the house for about two hours. She's kept herself busy with cleaning and doing laundry and avoiding me. I'm not sure that's what she's doing, but it sure as hell seems like it. Maybe, now that she's had some time to think about it, she's decided that our intimate moment earlier this morning was too much for her, and she doesn't want a repeat. Or, maybe she just doesn't want to risk her children walking in on us. Who knows? In any case, I'm out of projects and can't stall anymore.

She's in her bedroom, staring at her bed with glassy eyes.

"Emmy?"

Just the simple sound of her name causes her to start. She jumps back and lets out a squeal. I wasn't intentionally trying to sneak up on her, but the quality carpet and padding muffled my movements. She grabs her heart and giggles nervously.

I smile, too, although I'm not sure what all the fuss is about. What was she doing that made her so nervous in the first place?

"Sorry. I didn't mean to scare you."

She walks to me.

"I know. I think I'm just a little too jumpy with everything going on."

Her tone is a bit different than the way she usually speaks. *She's lying.* Although about what, I have no idea. It makes sense that she's jumpy, given everything that she's been through in the last few days. But, why is she lying about that?

"I'm finished with the locks. The keys are in the kitchen. I'm going to head back to my hotel room. Will you be okay here alone for a little while?"

She smiles again, more genuinely this time.

"Thank you so much for helping me today. Since you won't let me pay you for your time or the locks, please let me at least make you dinner tonight."

"No. I really want to take you out. I've made reservations and everything. I'll pick you up at six-thirty."

"Are you sure?"

"Yes. I'm sure. I really want to do this."

She leans up and kisses me lightly on my cheek. "See you tonight."

## Chapter Twenty-Eight

### Emmy

A huge sigh escapes as I fall backwards onto my bed.

*That was a close one.*

Jackson almost saw where I hide the Rutledge ring. I know that I can trust Jackson, but I still don't want him to know. *I don't want anyone to know.* I don't want anyone to suspect that it's even in my house. Let them think that it's in a safe deposit box somewhere—anywhere but here. Plus, Jackson will give me a hard time about keeping the ring here. The last thing I need is another lecture from him.

Jackson's taking me out to dinner tonight. My first date in almost twenty years. Of course, I almost had sex with him *before* our first date. My body flushes, remembering the feel of his body against mine as he carried me across the kitchen. Will we get the chance tonight? Based on my body's response, I sure hope so. Every time we get into something, we get interrupted. I definitely don't want to be interrupted again.

Hayes and Audrey come home around four o'clock and find me in the same position. Guess I drifted off. Easy to do with the little bits of sleep I've had the last couple of nights.

They're showered and ready to go before five, the scheduled time for Andrew to pick them up. I haven't showered or done anything to get ready for my date. Hayes and Audrey don't need to know that I have plans tonight.

"Are you going out tonight with Jackson?"

*So much for keeping my plans to myself.* Hayes's voice is curious but hopeful. Audrey looks up from her phone.

"Would it be okay with you if I did go out to dinner with Jackson?"

Hayes smiles.

"Yeah. He's great. So does that mean that you do have a date with him?"

"Yes, he's taking me out to dinner."

"Good. Stay out really late and have a good time."

Audrey smiles and resumes her texting.

"You know that Jackson is on his way to a job in California, right? This is just going to be one date. That's it."

Hayes nods. "Sure, but you should have as much fun with him as you can while he's here."

The doorbell rings. I hug each of them, planting a kiss on their cheeks. I'm still allowed to do that when it's only the three of us, or in this case, just their father. That's our deal. I can kiss them when we're alone as long as I don't try it in public.

They open the door and walk out, but the door doesn't close behind them. Andrew steps inside the house. He stands only about two steps from the door though and looks around warily.

"Is he here?"

"Do you mean Jackson?"

I know who he means, but it feels good to say Jackson's name in front of Andrew. *Maybe a little evil on my part but well-deserved as far as I'm concerned.*

"No. He's not here right now." *But he will be.*

Andrew's body visibly relaxes. "Do you have any idea what they were after when they broke in last night?"

"No."

I keep my answer short. It's too weird discussing this with Andrew. It would be better if he would just leave.

"It was the bracelet you were trying to sell on Monday, wasn't it? The one with the diamonds and sapphires?"

A sigh escapes. "Yes, Andrew. It's mine to sell. If you paid your fair share for child support, then I wouldn't have to sell my jewelry."

"I pay what the court deemed adequate, and I'm never late with a payment."

And his smugness is back, just like that—makes me want to hit him. Maybe it would be good if Jackson were here to deck him. Of course, Andrew wouldn't be saying any of this if Jackson were here. He would have crawled away like the chicken that he is.

"Goodbye, Andrew."

He opens his mouth to say something else, then closes it. He simply turns and walks out the door, closing it firmly behind him. I stand numbly in the foyer and watch Hayes and Audrey climb into his Mercedes. The kids are never thrilled about the time they have with Andrew, but he is their father, and visitation is short. They will be back before swim practice in the morning. It's that and every other weekend, not much time to spend with their *other* family. It's important for them to spend time with their father, even if he is a cheating asshole.

\*\*\*

Jackson arrives right on time. He's wearing khakis and a button down shirt that pairs well with my sundress. I didn't ask him where he's taking me, so I wasn't entirely sure what to wear. The dress I chose has a bright floral pattern in reds, pinks and blues—quite a color combination, I know, but it somehow works without being tacky. It has spaghetti straps and a flowing skirt that ends just above the knee. I chose my tan leather espadrilles that add two inches to my height. Two inches isn't much compared to his six-foot-three, but I'll take it. Most importantly—and I really hope this turns out to be important—I'm wearing an ivory lace bra and panties to match. No cotton tonight.

Jackson smiles approvingly when I answer the door. He steps inside, closes the door behind him, and then plants a kiss on me that takes my breath away. His large arms and hands engulf me. He backs me up until I hit the wall behind me and can't walk any further.

Just when I think that we might not be going out to dinner after all, he pulls back. His mouth looks amused, and his eyes are smiling and definitely a brighter blue than usual. He reaches behind me and removes my hair clip. My hair tumbles from the chignon I'd spent twenty minutes getting just right. Jackson brushes it back with his fingers and lightly kisses my bare shoulder.

"Much better."

The sound of the doorbell echoes through the house. *Who is it this time?*

A large sigh escapes me as I pull the door open. It's Marci. *Marci.* Almost the last person that I want to see. Her gaze moves away from me quickly, searching for Jackson. Her smile turns to beaming when she spots him. She stands a little straighter. Her double Ds pop to attention and do their best not to fall out of the tank top she's wearing. *Give me a break already*.

Jackson smiles. Marci giggles. *I think I'm going to throw up*.

"We were just on our way out. Is there something I can help you with, Marci?"

Her smile fades a touch, but that's probably because her eyes meet mine for a quick second before they move back to Jackson. *That's right. I'm still here.* This is my house after all.

"I heard about what happened last night, so I made you some brownies."

*Brownies? Really? Nothing like a home invasion to make me want baked goods.*

That's not fair, really. Would I be so angry about her stupid brownies if she hadn't made them only to have an excuse to stick her boobs in Jackson's face? She holds a foil-covered plate out in front of her. She's still gawking at Jackson. I take the plate from her and set it on the table next to me.

"Thank you, Marci. That was so thoughtful. I wish we could stay and chat, but Jackson and I have a reservation."

She pouts at my words. It's not a normal pout either, it's all sexy. Does she practice that move in a mirror? Did she have lip injections to get her lips to be so full?

"I guess I'll be going then. See you around, soon hopefully."

She says all of this to Jackson, which is not a

surprise at this point. She smiles, turns, and sashays towards her car. Her butt cheeks peek out of the frayed hem of her short shorts. I can't seem to pull my eyes away, so I can only imagine the effect the view has on Jackson. We both wave as Marci backs her car out of the driveway. Jackson's expression is amused.

"I *really* don't like her."

"Why not? She was so thoughtful to come by and check on you, and she made you brownies."

The anger is instantaneous. One look at Jackson, though, and I know he's just joking, a mischievous smile on his lips.

"That woman has never stopped by my house. She's only here to flaunt herself in front of you. She's ridiculous."

"No argument there."

Jackson leans in and plants a warm kiss on the base of my neck. Marci is magically forgotten.

I grab my purse, carefully locking up using my new front door key, and walk with Jackson to his truck. Anne smiles and waves from her yard two houses down. She appears to be picking up some sports equipment that was left outside, but I know she's just being nosy. It's been two years at least since she stopped picking up after her children. She makes them do it now, but apparently she makes an exception when it gives her an excuse to spy on me.

"So where are we going?"

"Liberty Tavern. Have you been there before?"

"No. I haven't. I tend to avoid the touristy places in the old part of town.

"Good. I researched the place, and it's just what I'm looking for—lots of antiques and the servers wear period costumes, just like at Disney."

"Uh-huh. Have you ever actually been to Disney?"

"No, but I've always wanted to go. Relax, Emmy. It will be fun."

He pulls my hand up to his mouth and plants a kiss on the back of it. The electricity shoots straight to my nether region.

"Thank you for letting me take you out."

## Chapter Twenty-Nine

### Jackson

Dinner is surprisingly good. The restaurant is as cheesy as promised, but the beef stew is delicious, and the company is amazing. Emmy is incredible. It's everything about her: the way that she smiles, the way she tucks an unruly hair behind her ear, the way that she lights up when she talks about Hayes and Audrey. *I have it bad*. This is what I wanted to feel with Katherine, but I didn't. There's no comparison. Everything is somehow magnified. But, I've known Emmy for less than forty-eight hours. How is it possible to feel like this so soon?

We skip dessert at the restaurant and have gelato from a street vendor instead. Emmy and I both order mango and walk along the paths that wind through the William and Mary campus. She points out the various buildings and landmarks along the way. A few students walk around the grounds, but the campus is mostly deserted during the summer. The evening is warm, but somehow it has lost the mugginess that was so prevalent earlier in the day. Emmy leads me to a quiet bench and pulls me down next to her. The sun is setting now, low in the sky, casting its last light on the brick buildings.

My gaze moves back to Emmy. In the time it's taken me to study my surroundings, her mouth has fallen from a content smile to a tight line. She's going through a lot—too much.

"I think you should leave tomorrow."

*That I wasn't expecting.* She keeps her focus trained ahead and doesn't look at me.

"Why would you say that? I don't want to leave tomorrow." I place my hand on hers. "Emmy, look at me." She slowly turns her head to face me. "Why?"

"Because I don't want to regret keeping you here. You belong in California. You've done so much for me already, and I will never forget you, but you have to go."

"Emmy, we all make choices that we regret, mistakes that we don't want to make again. I'm not leaving you here alone when you need me."

"But..." I wave my hand to cut her off.

"I told you that I was married once." She nods. "Katherine was a good woman and a good wife. I was a horrible husband."

I blink my eyes to keep them dry as years of unresolved guilt comes flooding over me.

*Why am I telling her this?*

She turns her body toward me. "I'm sure that you weren't."

"I was. We got married way too fast. I was barely out of training. We went to Vegas on vacation and thought it would be a lark to get married while we were there. It was a huge mistake. We weren't in love, at least not like we should have been. I worked constantly. She was home by herself, sometimes for weeks at a time. I told myself that it was worth it. I was a SEAL. There was always another mission, always more training. There were all kinds of things that took me away from home. She didn't like the time I spent away, and that's understandable. But she began to resent me for it. The more I was away, the more she complained, which made me want to stay away even more. After a while I realized that's what I was doing. I was avoiding her."

My story makes me sound like a complete shit, even to myself. Emmy's expression is blank. What does she think about my admission?

"Then Katherine got pregnant. She stopped yelling at me for being away. She was busy with preparations for the baby. It was a girl. She was so excited that she painted one of the bedrooms the most awful shade of pink."

Emmy sits a little straighter, waiting for the

outcome of the story.

"Then Katherine lost the baby at eight months." Emmy's intake of breath is sudden. She scoots closer to me and puts her arm around my shoulders.

"Oh, Jackson. I'm so sorry."

There's no comfort that she can give me to help me forget my own terrible actions.

"I was on a mission at the time. Word came through that Katherine was in the hospital. My commanding officer was amazing. He gave me the choice—to stay if I wanted or to go home to her. It should have been an easy decision. I should have run home to her as fast as I could, but I didn't." I look down at my lap, still feeling Emmy's piercing stare.

"I got to the hospital as Katherine was checking out. One look at her, and I knew that she'd lost our baby. Her parents were with her; they'd flown in from Oregon. Her father took me outside and read me the riot act. I deserved it. He told me in no uncertain terms that I was never to contact his daughter again. I wanted to tell him that I couldn't be there any sooner, but the lie wouldn't even form on my tongue. He was right. We said our goodbyes in front of her parents on the curb of the hospital. That's my biggest regret."

Emmy turns my chin to face her. My eyes are wet with tears. Emmy's crying as well, tears are streaming down her face.

"Where is Katherine now?"

"She's back in Oregon. She married a hops

farmer, and they have three children."

"It sounds like she has a good life. Maybe things worked out like they were supposed to."

"Maybe. I don't regret that we got a divorce—we shouldn't have gotten married in the first place—but she was my wife. She needed me then, and I should have been there for her. I should have been there for our baby."

Why am I still talking? Now that the words have started, they won't be stopped.

"We were going to name her Heidi."

"That's a pretty name."

"Katherine chose it." A heavy sigh leaves me. "My friend, Marco, found me sitting on a bench outside the hospital. I remember watching Katherine and her family get into a car and drive away. There was nothing else until Marco showed up. He was there to visit us. He took me back to his place and insisted I stay there with him and his wife for a while. I lasted three days there. It was a long enough time for him and a few of my buddies to disassemble the nursery. They took all of the baby stuff out of the room and repainted it white to match the rest of the rooms in the house. "

Emmy leans in and kisses my cheek softly.

"Marco is a great friend."

"The best. He's the one waiting for me in San Diego. He retired about six months ago and is getting very bored waiting for me." My gaze meets Emmy's and holds. "I don't want to go anymore. I need to be here with you now. You need me, and this is where I want to be."

"I do need you."

Emmy whispers the words, her meaning very clear.

"Let's go back to your house."

"No. Let's go to your hotel. Less chance of interruption. Let's have one amazing night together, and then you can ride off into the sunset. No regrets for either of us."

It would be an enormous regret leaving Emmy even after one amazing night, but I will argue with her about that later.

## Chapter Thirty

### Emmy

Jackson's shirt is the first thing to go. I begin working the buttons as soon as the door to his hotel room is closed. My hands are burning to touch his chest. He pulls a strap off my shoulder and kisses the spot where it rested. It's all I can do not to cry out. His lips are magic as they trail kisses to my neck and then up to my jaw.

Unbuttoning complete. He lets go of me long enough to allow the sleeves to slide down his arms. I take a moment to ogle Jackson's body. *Wowzers!* That's what I would say if I could form words, but instead, I'm completely speechless. Muscles are everywhere. My fingers move to his abdomen, touching carefully, as if there might literally be a spark. Andrew was fit, but nothing—and I mean *nothing*—like this. No more thoughts of Andrew—not hard to do because Jackson kisses me again, and all I can think of is Jackson.

My arms move around his neck as he deepens our kiss. His tongue explores and plunders, and I let him take all of me. I pull him closer. *I need him closer.* His hands move to my butt, and he lifts me up as my legs instinctively wrap around him, just like they did this morning.

*Only this time there will be no interruptions.*

He walks me to the bed and sets me down carefully. My eyes are now level with his belt buckle, so I begin working on that. His pants slide down in no time.

He smiles. I smile, too. I feel confident. I'm a little nervous to be with Jackson, but I'm not a young girl like I was the first time Andrew and I were together. I know what to do. I've said that there will be no regrets, and I meant it. This is my only night with Jackson, and I'm going to make it count.

He kneels down next to the bed as he slowly pushes the hem of my dress up my leg. A wicked smile comes to his face. *Okay, maybe now I'm going to panic.* He leans forward and licks me through the lace of my panties. Ripples of excitement shoot up through my body. He slides my panties down slowly, keeping his eyes locked on mine the entire time. He pulls me lower and places my legs over his shoulders. His amazing mouth does its thing, and staying quiet is no longer possible. He brings me to the edge of that magical cliff but doesn't let me fall over. Not yet. He steps out of his boxers and moves on top of me. Our bodies move together in perfect unison until we both begin to shudder. We utter one last long moan together as Jackson falls on top of me.

It should be uncomfortable with two hundred plus pounds of solid muscle lying on me. *Nope.* Not even a little. Jackson feels incredible. He slowly rolls off after a few minutes. We're both still catching our breath. He turns me to my side and unzips my sundress. He slowly undresses me and then throws my dress on the floor. I feel the heat of his gaze as he takes in each part of my body, beginning at my toes and slowly working his way up to my face. Jackson's smoldering eyes lock with mine. His arms move around me, and we're on to round two.

\*\*\*

We made love four times. *Four.* Let's just say, I don't think Jackson uses steroids to get all those muscles. Everything works just fine. No, much better than fine even. *Did I mention four times*? Are there records for this kind of thing? Andrew and I were lucky to do it once, and that was even back in the early days when we were young. Imagine what Jackson was like when he was young.

"How old are you?" The words pop out of my mouth. If you want to know the answer, then you have to ask the question, right?

"Forty-two. Why?"

My lips curve up into a smile. *Forty-two.*

It's four a.m. We're dressing so that Jackson can take me back home before the kids get there. Hayes's swim practice starts at seven. While I have no regrets about my night with Jackson, I can't advertise it to my children.

I sit down on the edge of the bed to slip on my shoes. Jackson, already dressed, sits down next to me. I smile and take his hand. His hand that works just as much magic as his mouth.

"I'm really glad that we had this time together before you have to leave."

His eyes widen. His shoulders slump.

"You can't want me to leave now."

Smile gone.

*Crap.*

"You have to go. That was our deal."

"That was your deal. I never agreed to it. How can you want me to leave after last night?"

"Because I'm not going to hold you back from your plans." How can I make him understand? *He has to go.*

"That's what Andrew did to me, and I'm not going to do that to you."

"Don't I get some say in this?"

*No. I'm doing this for your own good, you idiot.*

I stand, grab my purse, and walk out the door.

## Chapter Thirty-One

### Jackson

Emmy should have cracked by now. I am—totally cracking to pieces. Emmy's steel. She hasn't said a word the whole way back to her house. The silence is deafening and worsens with each passing minute. What can I say to make her see reality? When we finally park in her driveway, the weight of our situation is heavy on my chest making it difficult to even breathe.

"I'm sorry, Jackson. I can't regret you later. I can't hold you back from your dream."

"Well, I can't regret leaving you. Please let me stay."

*I don't care if I'm begging at this point. I don't*

*know what else to do.*

"How? Your friend Marco is waiting for you. Your future is in California. Mine is here."

"Come with me."

This time the words are not a surprise. *She feels so far away already.* I lean toward her across the cab of the truck and place my hand on hers. She pulls away.

"Goodbye, Jackson."

She chokes out the words. This is hard for Emmy, too. Can't she see that she doesn't need to protect me? She will never be a regret for me.

She opens the door, slides out of my truck, and moves up the walkway to her front door. My eyes follow her every move. How can she do this? Will she turn and look at me?

She does—just before she shoves her key into the lock. She turns, gives me a wistful smile, and then disappears into her house. I touch the handle of my door, knowing that this isn't over. I'm going to beg her to reconsider. Begging. How did I reach this point?

Emmy's scream pierces the early morning air.

I'm out of my truck and up the walkway in seconds. I push the door open and bound inside. The fancy foyer chandelier lights the area. Emmy stands at the edge of the living room.

Which is a total mess. No, more like complete devastation. The couch cushions have been ripped apart, stuffing spread all over the room. Tables are upended. Lamps lay busted on the floor.

Emmy is borderline hysterical, her breath comes out in audible wheezes. I grab hold of her shoulders and turn her body to face me.

"Listen to me."

*Am I getting through?* Her eyes flicker with understanding.

"Go lock yourself in my truck. Call 9-1-1. Then call Andrew and make sure Hayes and Audrey are okay. Do you understand?"

She nods, just barely. I walk her to the front door and watch her run disjointedly to my pickup. Once she's inside, I walk toward the back of the house. *Need to make sure these bastards aren't still here.* The doors to the china cabinet are hanging open. Cracked china litters the floor. The table and chairs are piled on the far side of the room, maybe to allow the Oriental rug to be moved out of its spot because it's rolled out of the way and thrown on top of the table.

The family room looks much like the living room. The leather furniture has been cut open, stuffing strewn around the room. A photo of Emmy and her family lies on its side under broken glass. It takes a considerable amount of effort to resist the urge to right it, but I know the importance of a clean crime scene.

*Who did this?*

A gasp escapes as I make the turn into the kitchen. The cabinets are open. Broken dishes and food cover the countertops, table, and floor. Sure I've seen much worse in my life—I've been in some major hell holes—but this is Emmy's house. These things have personal meaning and Emmy is going to lose it. And soon, apparently, because I hear her come through the front door. Her sandals click across the wood floor of the foyer. The sound changes. *Shit!*

She's going up the stairs.

*The intruders could still be up there.*

I race up the second set of stairs off the kitchen in the hopes that it will be faster. She's down the hall coming towards me.

"Emmy, wait. I haven't checked up here yet."

She looks away from me and hurries through the double doors into her bedroom. I rush after her and catch her just in time to hear her scream.

"*No!*"

She leans over the bed, her fingers frantically searching a hole that's been cut into the mattress. It's different than the other cuts and slashes around the house. This hole is cut in a neat three-inch square. She falls into a sitting position and begins crying.

I kneel down beside her.

"Hayes and Audrey. Are they okay?"

She nods. Relief courses through me. That's the most important thing. The rest of this is just stuff. It can be replaced.

I wrap my arms around her and pull her to me.

Sobs rack her body. I hold her tightly and wait.

\*\*\*

Sirens announce the arrival of the police. From the sound of things, they sent more than one car this time.

"Let's go down and talk to them."

Emmy nods and allows me to pull her to a standing position. With my arm wrapped around her, we walk down the hallway and then down the front stairs. We arrive in the foyer just as the policemen are walking inside. There are four patrolmen. All young men this time. The young ones probably get the night shift.

We all introduce ourselves. I stay close to Emmy. She's barely keeping it together. Her eyes fill with tears, she wipes them with the back of her hand, and they fill again. She stands to the side, her arms hugged in front of her. She's always such a good hostess, but she has nowhere to invite the officers to sit and nothing to offer them to drink.

"Detectives Marshall and Patterson are on their way. We'll check out the scene until they arrive. Was there anything that was taken that you've noticed so far?"

"Yes, my Rutledge ring."

## Chapter Thirty-Two

### Emmy

*This is what I get.*

When I made that cut-out in my mattress, I thought I was just the smartest person alive. Who would think to unzip the pillow top and inspect the mattress? People who know what they're doing, that's who.

It's just shameful. The most expensive thing I own, well owned, and now it's gone.

Jackson ushers me outside and sits down with me on the front steps.

"I guess that's where you kept the ring? In that hole in your mattress?" I nod. It's not a secret anymore. "Why?"

More tears leak from my eyes.

"I was being spiteful. I removed the ring from the safe deposit box because I didn't want Carson to get her smarmy hands on it. My jewelry was the one part of my divorce settlement that didn't go Andrew's way. He tried hard to get that ring back from me so that he could give it to Carson. I wasn't going to let that happen, so I hid it in what I thought was an ingenious hiding spot. Guess not."

"Is it insured?"

Insured. *Yes!* Excitement and hope fill me.

"Oh my gosh. Do you know what this means?"

Jackson's forehead wrinkles as he studies me. His head tilts slightly.

"I would never have sold that ring, or at least not until we were on the brink of starvation. There was a clause that said if I ever wanted to sell it, that I had to offer it to Andrew and his family first. Then *she* would end up with it after all. *But*, if they can't recover the ring, then I will get the insurance money, and I'll have the money I need to get settled in a new house."

I'm smiling now. Tears are still falling down my cheeks, but I think that maybe they've switched to happy tears, tears of relief.

*Okay. Maybe I'm losing it.*

*Maybe I've lost it already.*

Jackson's eyes widen.

"I see where you're going with this, but you might want to play down your excitement. That attitude would not go over well with the cops inside."

"Probably not, but you see what I mean, right? This might turn out to be just what I needed."

"Emmy, your home was violated, and your belongings were completely destroyed."

"You're right." *He is right.* "But is it so bad to find some kind of good in all of this?"

"Honestly, I don't even know right now. You've been through so much, and the last thing I'm going to do is judge you. But, I do know that you can't be talking about how the ring being stolen solves your money problems."

"Yeah. It's too early to know how that will work out anyway. The ring is one of a kind. Whoever stole it can't just pawn it. It's too recognizable. It might turn up after all." A big sigh escapes. "How did the intruders get inside the house? Can you tell?"

"I don't know. There are no broken windows, at least that I saw, but we haven't been through the entire house. Maybe they picked the lock this time."

Detectives Patterson and Marshall pull up to the curb and hop out of their car. Agent Marshall yawns as they walk towards us. They had to be woken up at this hour. Even early risers would be just getting up, but they sure got here fast. Jackson stands and meets them halfway down the driveway.

"You're here at this time of the morning?"

Detective Marshall's eyebrows rise knowingly as he asks the question. Normally, I would be embarrassed by that comment, but not today. There's way too much on my mind for that to even be a factor.

"I took Emmy out to dinner and then we spent some time at my hotel." Jackson pauses as if to allow time for Detective Marshall to fill in the blanks himself. "When I brought Emmy home this morning, we found that her house had been ransacked. It's a mess in there."

"Is the bracelet still there?"

"I don't know. We were only inside for a few minutes. We know that her vintage Rutledge ring is gone."

They stop walking now that they've reached us.

Agent Patterson speaks, "You're really having a bad week, Ms. Bennett."

What can I say to that? *This is the week from hell.*

Detective Marshall gives his partner a quick glare that I catch even though I think he's trying to be subtle about it.

"You two wait here while we look around. We'll be back shortly to ask you some questions."

\*\*\*

"Ms. Bennett, can you please come inside with us?"

Detective Marshall looks at me with kind blue eyes. Jackson's right. He wouldn't be so caring if he knew that I was just celebrating the thought of the insurance money.

"Let's walk through the house to see if you can determine if anything else was stolen. It will take going through all this mess to know for sure, but let's give it a preliminary look-see."

The mess. Ugh. Do I have to clean that up?

Jackson and I follow Detectives Marshall and Patterson into the house. There are crime scene people everywhere, taking notes, dusting for fingerprints. We weave in and out of their way and try not to disturb the mess on the floor as we walk through the first level. How can I possibly tell if anything's missing? Our home is a total wreck.

The large screen television is somehow intact, and that's the thing that has the most value on this floor. We should have started in my bedroom since I know everyone wants to know if the diamond and sapphire bracelet is missing. The detectives ask question after question as we work our way through the rooms. Detective Patterson takes many notes. We finally head upstairs.

I always thought that Hayes and Audrey's bedrooms were a mess, but what greets me is a whole new level of disaster. Jackson places his hand on the small of my back for support. His warmth is comforting, and it's nice, but truthfully, I don't need it. Seeing Hayes's swim trophies in a pile on the floor —many of them broken—and Audrey's stuffed animals sliced up, stuffing pulled out. *It's too much.*

Anger pumps through me. By the time we make

it to my bedroom, I'm ready to find the people who did this and kick their asses myself. My dressers and end tables are again covered in fingerprint powder. You'd think that seeing the powder covering my dressers and end tables just yesterday would lessen the shock of seeing it again. *It doesn't*. The jewelry drawer—the thin one at the top of my dresser is open and empty.

"What was in there?" Detective Marshall asks.

"Nothing of value, at least to anyone else. It was mostly costume jewelry, although there were a few favorites. I kept the expensive jewelry, including the bracelet, in the safe in my closet."

"That's what we figured. The safe is gone. All that's left of it is a square indentation in the carpet."

"Gone? They took the whole thing?"

I walk into the closet and see for myself. It really is gone.

"There had to be a whole crew in here then. That thing weighed a ton—maybe literally. It took Andrew and three friends to carry that thing up here."

Detective Patterson writes something in her notebook.

"And the Rutledge ring? Where was that?"

I walk back to the bed and show them my secret spot that wasn't so secret after all.

"We'll have more questions in a bit. For now, why don't you two go back outside?"

***

Jackson and I move to the deck in the back of the house for privacy—too many curious looks from neighbors walking their dogs or jogging. There are several police cars and a couple crime scene vans parked out front. It's quite a show.

Vanessa arrives at six-thirty. She's wearing a green denim skirt and coordinating sweater. For her, this is casual, although she's perfectly accessorized, so it had to take some effort. She just doesn't like people to think it did. She wants everyone to think that she wakes up perfectly pressed and made-up every morning. The look of pity on her face makes me cringe. Sure, my life has been a mess lately, but pity is one thing that I can't stand.

"Emmy, my dear. You poor thing." *Ugh*. So not what I need right now. I stand to greet her. She does her usual hug with the perfunctory kiss on the cheek, except this time she actually kisses my cheek.

"You remember Jackson."

Jackson holds out his hand for a shake but doesn't get one. He holds his arm out for a couple seconds and then lets it drop. *What the heck?* Vanessa is all about manners. Her ignoring Jackson's handshake isn't like her at all.

"Emmy, would it be possible for me to speak with you *alone*?"

Jackson looks to me for guidance. His eyes show understanding, but his creased brow shows annoyance—a strange combination.

"It's okay, Jackson. Can you give us a few minutes?"

"I'll be out front if you need me."

He steps off the deck and walks around towards the front of the house.

Vanessa's expression turns even more serious.

"Let's sit down."

I fall back down into the same chair. Vanessa sits in the one next to me and covers my hands with hers. *What's this all about?* She leans forward.

"Emmy, dear, I'm afraid that I have some very bad news for you."

My empty stomach churns in anticipation. The kids are fine. What else could have Vanessa acting like this?

"I know that I overstepped my bounds, and I'm sorry, but I was only looking out for you."

*Would she just get on with it already?*

"What is it, Vanessa?"

"I did some checking on your friend, Mr. Jackson."

A low whistle escapes from my ears. That's what it feels like anyway. Like a valve was released so that my head doesn't explode from the instant anger pressing on my insides. I pull my hands away from hers.

"You had no right to do that."

"I know. I know. It just seemed like too much of a coincidence, that he came into your life just as all these *unpleasant things* began happening. How much do you know about him?"

"Enough to know that he's a good man. He has *nothing* to do with this mess."

"He might. Just hear me out. Please."

I lean back in my chair, cross my arms in front of me, and steel myself for whatever lie Vanessa is about to tell me. There's nothing she can say that will change my mind about Jackson.

"Go ahead. What did you find out?"

"He's divorced."

A whoosh of breath escapes.

"*I'm divorced*. That isn't a crime, and besides, he told me that himself."

"Just bear with me." She sighs herself, as if it's difficult for her to speak the next words.

"He was arrested last year for breaking and entering. The charges were dropped, but it kind of goes hand in hand with what's been happening here."

"The charges were dropped. I'm sure there's a reasonable explanation." *Please, God, let there be a reasonable explanation.*

"My investigator had to dig deep to find this information. The records explain that he and a friend of his, Neil Smith, were involved in a crime ring in Norfolk. Your friend, Jackson, even spent some time in the Navy jail."

"But the charges were dropped, so he was acquitted."

"Maybe he was guilty, and he got off. He hasn't

told you anything about this? It seems like something he should have mentioned considering everything that's been happening to you."

I don't answer, but my non-answer is answer enough.

"Maybe he's working with someone now to rob you. Think about it. They saw the ad on-line that stated you wanted to sell the bracelet. They decided to see what else you have worth taking. They needed someone to work on the inside, so he got to know you so that he could see what else there is to take. It's not a stretch to get there."

*I disagree.*

"Thank you for sharing this information. I know that you mean well, but I don't want to hear any more."

I stand up to make it perfectly clear that this conversation is over. Vanessa meant well with her intrusion—I really want to believe that she did—but this is none of her business. She just met Jackson and isn't willing to give him a chance, much like she wasn't willing to give me a chance when she first met me. It took her years to be more than civil to me. She just doesn't get it. *Geez. Did she do a background check on me, too, when I started dating Andrew? Probably.*

Vanessa stands, places her hands on my shoulders, and squeezes.

"Please think about what I've told you. Ask Jackson about it if you want to. Just please don't be alone with him when you do. I'm truly disappointed that the police have not come up with this information on their own."

"Maybe they did, but they don't see him as a threat. Maybe they came to a different conclusion."

"Maybe. Just be careful, Emmy."

She pulls me to her for a real hug. She holds me tightly in her arms for several long seconds. In some ways, her hug is more shocking than the words she told me. She lets me go and walks around the front of the house.

## Chapter Thirty-Three

### Jackson

"Vanessa looked like she was on a mission. What did she want?" Emmy's skin is a pale white, and she looks completely drained. No point in beating around the bush. She steps toward me, and I wrap my arms around her. I inhale deeply and pull her scent into my lungs. She still smells wonderful even after the night we had together. Emmy leans back slightly. Her eyes meet mine.

"She wanted to talk about you, actually. She hired someone to investigate you. She wanted to share with me what she found."

"I can guess what she *found*. She learned that I was arrested, right?"

Emmy jumps backwards, out of my embrace. My arms fall to the side. *Shit*.

"Why didn't you tell me?" Emmy's gaze moves over my face, studying me as if seeing me for the first time.

*I should have told her*.

"There's more to this story. Let me tell you my side."

"Something that big, and you didn't mention it when you were telling me about your regrets?"

"It's true, but the reason that I didn't tell you about it then is that I don't regret it." Emmy's jaw drops. "I would have gotten there eventually. I've only known you for two days, and we've had more important things to talk about."

"Why would you keep something like that a secret?"

"Why would you?" Detective Marshall walks through the back door of the house and steps onto the deck. "I called several of your associates the other day in order to get to the truth myself. I felt confident that you were on the up and up. However, recent information has made me doubt the validity of what your Navy buddies said about you."

Detective Patterson and two uniformed officers come around the house and stand in the grass at the base of the steps that lead down from the deck.

"What kind of information?" I want to know, but Emmy beat me to it.

"Mr. Jackson, I will tell you now that we plan to

take you in for questioning based on this information. Will you cooperate and come willingly? From what I've heard about you, you probably could take us out, but there's no telling how much jail time you would get for police brutality."

"Of course I'll go with you for questioning. I have *never* hit a policeman, and I never intend to."

Anger wells up inside me. My teeth are clinched. I'm pretty sure I spoke that sentence without moving my lips.

Detective Marshall is visibly relieved at my words, but the two policemen keep their hands on their holsters. Emmy's expression is frantic.

"What is this information that is so damning to me? Would someone please tell me?"

Detective Marshall holds a single sheet of paper and turns it so that Emmy and I can both see it. It's a photo, likely taken from the security camera of one of the local businesses. It's a photo of me with Smitty. Emmy looks at me as if I can give her the reason why this picture is important. No idea.

"That's a photo of me and my friend, Smitty. We had lunch together on Monday. I told you about that already. What does that have to do with anything?"

"Your friend Smitty, Neil Smith, was identified by both Jose Martinez and Manuel Castro as the man who hired them to rob Ms. Bennett."

My attention is solely on Emmy. The remaining color leaves her face, leaving her complexion a ghostly white. She plops down into a chair behind her. Thank goodness it was there to catch her—don't want another fainting episode.

This is bad.

*Really bad.*

"Fuck you, Smitty."

The words come out as a harsh whisper as the realization hits me. Smitty used me. He picked that time for lunch so that I would be his alibi. Then there was that stupid phone call the other night. He was getting information about the case, using me to learn what he could. My gut was telling me something was wrong, and I ignored it.

"Smitty told me that he was clean. He promised me that he wasn't doing anything illegal. He has a wife and a job on campus. Is that not true?"

"Technically, both those things are true. However, his wife and his boss haven't seen him for more than twenty-four hours. He's likely skipped town and left you high and dry."

"What do you mean *left me high and dry*? You can't think that I had anything to do with what's been happening to Emmy."

"Are you going to deny your involvement? Or, are you going to tell me that the fact that you know the mastermind behind the robberies, and you happened to meet the victim during the robbery, is a complete coincidence?"

"That's exactly what I'm saying."

Emmy's crying now. She's looking down at the deck, but it's easy to see the tears as they fall.

*I am screwed.*

It takes only two steps to reach her. The officers both draw their weapons—I guess because of my sudden movement. I freeze and turn toward them.

"I will go willingly and answer all your questions. Just give me a second."

Detective Marshall gives me a slight nod of his head. That's all the permission I need.

I kneel down in front of Emmy. I don't take her hands, and I don't draw her to me—she wouldn't want me to touch her. She has to see my eyes. She has to see the truth in them.

"Emmy, I had nothing to do with whatever shit Smitty is into this time. I'm not going to say that he's innocent—I can't go that far. I thought he had cleaned up his act. Know though, that I had nothing to do with this. I swear."

Emmy's chestnut eyes meet mine in a piercing stare. She's fighting back. She's letting me know that she's not going to let me hurt her. But, I already have.

"You kept all of this a secret from me. How can being arrested not be a regret? Our discussion last night would have been the perfect time to bring it up. You intentionally kept it from me. There's no telling what else you're keeping from me. I don't want to hear anything else you have to say."

"I'm going to go with the detectives now so that they can ask me all the questions they need to. They won't keep me, because I'm innocent. When I get back, I will explain everything. I promise. You're right that I should have told you about this already, but you're wrong about one thing. What I did to get arrested was not something that I regret. If I were in that situation again, I would do exactly the same thing."

## Chapter Thirty-Four

*Emmy*

Jackson let the policeman handcuff him. In his case, I think it was just a formality. Jackson's probably badass enough to whip their butts handcuffed, but he went quietly, just as he'd promised. Someone must have gotten Anne for me—or knowing her, they found her loitering in my driveway. She comes around the house just as Jackson and the detectives walk away.

"You poor thing."

She pulls me into a hug. I wanted to poke Vanessa's eyes out when she said those words, but somehow they sound different coming from my good friend. I pull away and gesture for Anne to sit down. I take the same chair.

"I saw Jackson being led away in handcuffs. Did he hurt you?"

"No." *Not physically anyway.*

"*Thank God.* Did he do this to your house?"

"No."

"Well, what did he do?"

"Broke my heart, for one thing."

More tears want to escape, but there are no more. She squeezes my hand. My stomach churns as my mind works through the details. Jackson seems so trustworthy. I can't believe that he would do this to me, but how can he possibly not regret being arrested?

Hope rounds the corner of the house now. "Have no fear. The cavalry's here."

She walks up onto the deck and places a cardboard container that holds three large coffees on the table. She rummages in her large purse, removes a brown bottle, and pours a hefty amount of caramel-colored liquid into the coffees.

"Getting me liquored up at seven a.m.? Perfect."

"I haven't heard the latest updates, but when Anne called and said the police were at your house, I figured Kahlua was in order." I take a large sip of my coffee. Delicious, even on my empty stomach. "Now, if I missed the update about what in the world is going on here, you'll just have to start over."

I had previously kept the scarier parts of my story from them, especially from Anne, but I don't any longer. I tell them everything. I tell them about how I tried to sell my bracelet and how Jackson saved me, I tell them about finding someone in our house, and I tell them about how someone destroyed everything while looking for my jewelry. I tell them about Jackson, too, and about how much I've grown to care for him, even in such a short amount of time. *I slept with him.* I told myself that I wouldn't regret our night together. What if he really is in on it?

"Maybe he actually is innocent. He told you that he could explain." Hope seems…well…hopeful.

"I want to believe him, and I feel like he's telling the truth, but at the same time, I don't see how it's possible. How can he not regret something that put him in jail? It makes more sense that he's involved. Maybe Jackson cased out the place while he was here. He saw me near the bed yesterday. He may have guessed that's where the ring was hidden. He knew about the Rutledge ring. We even talked about how much it was worth."

"If that were the case, then the thieves would have looked there first. They wouldn't have had to go to the trouble of destroying the rest of your house to look for it. Did he know that you had the ring in the house?"

"No. No one knew that, but they must have suspected it since they searched so thoroughly. If they just wanted my jewelry, they could have taken the safe and run. There wasn't a ton in it of value, but there were a few pricey pieces. The bracelet was in it. There's another thing, too. I really wanted to cook Jackson dinner last night, but he insisted that we go out. He kept me out of the house for hours, probably so that his accomplices could search the house for all my valuables."

*That doesn't feel right.*

"He still didn't know that the ring was in your house. Did they take anything else?"

"Yes. They took all my jewelry. The only jewelry I have left is what I'm wearing right now."

I feel their gaze on me as they check it out. My entire collection now consists of a matching sterling silver necklace, earrings, and bracelet. My palm slaps against my forehead.

"There's another thing, too. Jackson changed the locks. He had the keys."

I swallow hard to keep down the bile that's working its way up my throat. *Be strong.*

Hope's hand finds mine. She squeezes it tightly. Tears are in her eyes as well.

"What do you feel in your heart? Do you believe him?"

"I do believe him. Am I an idiot?" Tears well up in my eyes again. Anne hands me a napkin that I use to wipe my eyes. "Do I believe him because he's innocent or because I spent the night with him? I don't know if I can trust myself. It's not like I have a good record for trusting the right people. Look what Andrew did to me."

"Andrew is an ass. Don't let him ruin your ability to trust Jackson."

"You're right." *She is right.* Plus, I just can't imagine a world where Jackson isn't the good guy.

***

"Mom?"

Hayes steps around the house now. A groan involuntarily slips from my throat. *He doesn't need to see me like this.*

"They said you were back here. They wouldn't let me in the house. What's going on?"

He jogs toward us. I meet him at the top of the deck stairs, and I bring him in for a quick hug. He's shirtless, wearing only his swim trunks and flip flops. His hair is wet.

"You aren't supposed to be here."

*He's not.* He's supposed to be at swim practice and then spending the day with Carson. She'd graciously offered to keep Hayes and Audrey for the day so that they didn't have to see the police going through the house. I hate to admit it to myself, but it was nice of her to offer.

"Dad wouldn't tell me what's going on."

"Does he know where you are?"

"No. I told the coach that I was going to the bathroom, but I walked here instead. Mom, tell me what happened. Where's Jackson?"

Hayes's eyes widen, the fear evident. I didn't

school my expression enough at the mention of Jackson's name. I plaster a smile on my face, but it's too late. I'm sure he can tell that I've been crying.

"I'll tell you, but first you have to text your dad and Carson and let them know where you are."

"I left my phone."

*That is a surprise.* Hayes wanted to get here so badly, he left his phone behind. Somehow that makes my smile a bit more real. I pull him to me for another hug. Hope hands Hayes her phone, and he begins texting away.

"We're going to go ahead and go. You two need a chance to talk." Anne stands. Hope does the same. She begins gathering the empty coffee cups from the table.

"I will check on you later. You know where I am if you need me sooner. I'm not going anywhere today."

She smiles, gives me a tight squeeze, and cuts through the neighbor's yard towards her house.

Hope hugs me, too. "I love you. Let me know if there's anything that I can do."

"You can *not* fire me. I won't be at work again today."

Hope chuckles. "I can handle that. Don't you even think about work today."

"Can you handle talking to Professor McDuff about not failing me? I missed class last night to go on my date with Jackson, I'm way behind on my homework, and I have no brain power left with which to do it."

"If we need to, but I'm sure he'll be willing to work something out. Take all the time you need."

"Thank you, Hope. I don't know what I'd do without you."

***

"Did Jackson do this to our house?"

Hayes's eyes search mine for answers.

"I don't think so, but the police are asking him some questions about it just to be sure."

"You can tell me what happened, you know. I'm not a kid anymore."

I take in Hayes's six-foot physique. How did he get so tall when I'm so short? He's going to be taller than Andrew. Sure he's a bit on the skinny side, but he is filling out. *He chased a criminal out of our house.*

*How did my baby turn into this young man?*

"I'd rather not go through all the details of what's been happening." Hayes moves to protest. I shake my head and hold up my hand to silence him. "It's not because I think you're a kid. To start with, I don't have all the answers. And, all of this is very fresh. I brought Jackson into our home and trusted him so readily. What if I made a mistake? Sons are not supposed to know that their mothers worry about making mistakes."

*Hayes also doesn't need to know that our financial situation is dire enough that I'm trying to sell jewelry to pay bills or that I was held at gunpoint.*

"It will work out, Mom. I trust him." I scoot my chair closer to Hayes's and squeeze his shoulder. "Don't give up on him until you're sure. Jackson makes you happy. You haven't been that happy since way before Dad left."

A large sigh escapes as Hayes hugs me to him.

## Chapter Thirty-Five

## Jackson

"Run through your story again. How the hell do you expect us to believe that you were with your friend, Mr. Smith, minutes before Ms. Bennett was attacked, and yet you had nothing to do with it? It took some doing, but Castro and Martinez ratted Smith out. You've been in trouble with Smith before. I'm not buying your innocent act anymore."

We're in an interrogation room at the police station where we've been for a while. There's no clock, so there's no telling how long we've been at it, really. It's small and uncomfortable by design, at least for a normal person. I'm a SEAL. I've seen worse conditions, so this is nothing. They don't need to know that though. They also don't need to know that I suspected Smitty of wrongdoing.

Detective Marshall is doing the talking. He's no longer playing the good cop that I've seen until this point. He's taken on the role of no-nonsense hard ass. Patterson is still taking notes. Hopefully, she's taking notes as much on how to interrogate and not just on what I'm saying in here. She's enthusiastic enough, but she could use some work on her people skills.

"We have a picture of you with the alleged mastermind. How do you explain that?"

Big sigh. We've been over this enough for me to seriously lose my patience. This is all part of their interrogation plan, and it normally wouldn't bother me. I might even find it funny, except that Emmy is out there thinking that I'm the bad guy, and *I am not the bad guy*.

"Smitty's an old Navy buddy. We do have a criminal past together, sort of. All of the guys on my team are close. I'm not going so far as to say that we're all best friends, but my life was often in their hands. There's a lot of trust there, and with that, comes a responsibility. We take care of each other." Detective Marshall nods and waits for me to continue. "There was an incident that happened on one of our missions. Smitty felt responsible. He was, but it was a mistake. He wanted to leave the Navy when his tour was up, but I talked him into re-enlisting. Then, not two months later, he was shot.

I'm not the one who shot him, but I feel the guilt anyway. If he'd been working as a civilian, the likelihood of getting shot would have been a hell of a lot less. He ended up getting out on a medical discharge. I guess he was meant to be out of the Navy at that point."

"At first we still hung out together. Little by little, Smitty became distant, started suffering from Post-Traumatic Stress Disorder. I was gone quite a bit, so I didn't notice how bad it was or that he was self-medicating to take the edge off. I found that out when I went to visit him about a year ago. I parked across the street from his house in time to watch a car pull into his driveway. Smitty ran out of the house, jumped in the car, and it sped off. I followed them and caught him and this other guy robbing a house. The other guy was younger than Smitty—mid-twenties I'd say. He picked the lock to gain access. I was so pissed that I wasn't thinking straight. I jumped out of my truck and went into the house after them. I *should have* called the police at that point, but I didn't. You should have seen Smitty's face when he saw me. He started clamoring excuses. The other guy pulled a gun on both of us, thinking it was some kind of double cross or something. I really don't know what I was thinking. I was just so let down that Smitty could do something like that. He swore that it was the first time he'd done anything criminal, and I believed him. Not sure I believe him anymore."

"How did you get caught?"

Detective Marshall is soaking up every word. He's very interested in what I have to say, but I can't tell if he believes me.

"That's just how the police found us. They saw the other guy had the gun trained on Smitty and me. We were all hauled in for questioning. I told the complete truth, but I also stuck up for Smitty. I played up his PTSD, which I know was the reason behind his behavior. If Smitty hadn't been taking drugs, he never would have attempted to rob anyone. That wasn't a lie. I didn't lie to the police then, and I'm definitely not lying now. The whole thing just compounded my guilt. If I hadn't talked him into re-enlisting, then he wouldn't have been shot. If he hadn't been shot, then he wouldn't have PTSD, he wouldn't have started doing drugs and hanging out with such lowlifes, and ending up robbing someone's house."

"That matches what the Norfolk detectives told us this morning."

It's the truth, so it should match, but it's still a relief to see Detective Marshall's body relax a little. He believes me. Not sure about Detective Patterson. She's stiff even when she's relaxed.

"Smitty got off. I thought that I was doing the right thing for him. I believed him when he said that it was the first time he'd ever done anything criminal. He and his wife moved to Williamsburg right after for a fresh start. I've called him every week to check in on him. Our lunch on Monday was the first time I'd seen him in person since last year. I don't know when I will be back on the east coast, and I was driving through Williamsburg on my way to San Diego. I have always wanted to check out the old town but never had, even though I was living only an hour away. This is the same stuff I told you before. It's not going to change because it's the truth."

Frustration pulses through my body in waves.

"Look, I told you from the beginning that I had a late lunch with a friend. Smitty was that friend. I gave you his name the first time I met you. If I were trying to hide something, would I have been so open about our friendship?"

A huge sigh escapes me. *What do I have to do to make them see?*

"It was when we were saying goodbye outside the restaurant that I saw Emmy for the first time. She's gorgeous. You know that I couldn't miss her, but I also couldn't miss how nervous she was, so I followed her. That's what I told you before, and that's exactly how it happened."

Marshall's shoulders dip just a little. He believes me.

"It's an incredible coincidence, don't you think?"

"Absolutely. From everything Smitty had been telling me, I thought that he'd been sticking to his promise to stay clean. He told me that he works nights as a security guard on campus. That is why we didn't meet until two-thirty for lunch. He sleeps until then every day. I think now that he wanted to meet me then to have a solid alibi. Emmy was late for her meeting. She threw off the timeline."

Marshall sighs heavily.

"Mr. Smith did have a security job on campus. However, he hasn't been to work since Sunday evening. It's like he had lunch with you and then bailed. Did you discuss anything during your time together that could have scared him off?"

"No. I asked him some questions about his life, but mostly we were shooting shit about the Navy. We had a lot of good times together despite the bad ones. Have you been to his house, talked to his wife?"

"Yes. She's a mess because of all this. She says she has no idea where he is. We believe her. Have you spoken with him since your lunch on Monday?"

"Smitty called me late Tuesday night. He said that he'd heard about what had happened and was calling to check on me. He told me that he was calling me from work, but I guess that was a lie. He had very little to say. He was surprised that I was still in town, but at that time, I was supposed to be leaving the next morning."

"Why didn't you leave then?"

"That was the night Emmy's house was broken into...the first time. I couldn't leave her after that. The longer I stay here, the less I want to leave at all. How did they get into the house?"

"So far, it looks like they used a key, or they knew the code for the garage."

My eyes widen. "That's impossible. I changed all the locks and the garage code just yesterday. The only people who had the new keys and codes were Emmy, Hayes, and Audrey."

"What did you do with the new keys?"

"I gave all of the keys to Emmy. They were sitting on her kitchen counter when I left in the afternoon, all of them."

"How do we know that you didn't make a copy for yourself or one for your accomplice?"

"I never left, so I wouldn't have been able to make a copy."

"You could have made a mold of the key or copied it some other way. I'm sure you SEALs have a few tricks."

"I didn't. I'm a civilian now. I don't carry those kinds of tools around with me. The doors required different types of locks, so I was unable to buy them with matching keys. Two keys came with each lock set. So, there were four keys all together, and all four of them were sitting on the kitchen counter when I left."

"You could have given the new garage code to an accomplice."

"But. I. Didn't."

"What about the ex-husband that we met yesterday? Were there any other visitors yesterday afternoon?"

"His mother came by as well. She brought us lunch, not long after you left. I hadn't started working yet though, so the lock packages were both unopened. Neither of them could have gotten their hands on the keys during those visits."

"What about after that?"

"I left Emmy's house around three and went back to my hotel until just before six-thirty, when I went back to pick up Emmy for dinner. One of Emmy's neighbors, a woman named Marci, can verify the time. She came by then to drop off some brownies. She never went into the house. Emmy's friend, Anne, can verify the time, too. She was outside in her driveway and saw us leave for dinner."

"The Bennett children were with their father and step-mother last night?"

"Yes."

"Did they have one of the new keys with them?"

"I don't know. Emmy may have given them one. I wasn't there when their father came to pick them up."

Marshall and Patterson exchange a look. Guess they'll be talking to Andrew. Could Andrew do something like this? He is a first-rate asshole, but that doesn't make him a criminal.

"I still can't believe that Smitty is involved in this. You're sure that these guys are telling the truth?"

"It looks like it, and it doesn't help that your friend skipped town. That makes him look even more guilty."

"I wanted him to make a good life for himself, and I'm not going to give up on him even if he is a complete screw-up. Maybe I was wrong to bail him out last time. Maybe some jail time is what he needs to get his shit together."

Marshall's eyes have softened now. There's no doubt now about his feelings.

"Are you going to charge me? Emmy probably hates my guts right now. Can I please get back to her and explain?"

"Yeah. I'll drive you there myself." Marshall stands and looks me in the eye. "We will release you, but you have to stay in Williamsburg. If we find that one shred of what you told us is untrue, you'll go to jail."

"Understood." I don't want to leave town anyway.

## Chapter Thirty-Six

### Emmy

"Mommy? Are you okay?" Audrey bounds up the steps and onto the deck. She's wearing her swimsuit and shorts. Her wet hair is pulled back in a ponytail. She stayed for her practice. I stand and hug her to me, wetness and all.

"Are you, Emmy? Is there anything that I can do?"

Andrew is right behind her. His blue eyes echo the sincerity in his tone. He's dressed more casually today—plaid shorts, a blue golf shirt, and leather loafers—guess he's skipping work. That's nice actually, given the circumstances. Or, maybe Carson didn't want to be left alone with Hayes and Audrey for the whole day. My head shakes at the thought.

That isn't kind, and as much as I dislike both of them, I have bigger things to worry about right now.

"No, thank you. At this point, I just need the police to get whatever evidence they need and leave so that I can get this mess cleaned up. Most of our furniture is ruined, so at least that makes the clean-up easier."

I'm not crying—at least not yet—but a quick sob escapes from my throat. I take a deep breath and concentrate on not losing it in front of Hayes and Audrey. They don't need to see me having a meltdown. A few deep breaths do the trick.

"Then, once I get everything cleaned up, I'm going to put the house on the market. It's time for us to move."

Andrew's face pales. His body stiffens.

"You can't take the kids away. That was part of the settlement."

Big sigh.

"I'm not moving out of town." *You moron.* "I can't afford to live in this house anymore. You know that the divorce settlement wasn't exactly *beneficial* to me." I reign in my words and flatten my tone. I've never spoken negatively about Andrew in front of the children. I'm not going to start now. And to think I was just having semi-nice thoughts about him and Carson only moments ago.

"Does this mean that we can't move to California with Jackson?" All eyes turn to Audrey.

"How did you know about that?"

Audrey turns her body away from Andrew to face me. Her eyes tip downward.

"I was just hoping that we might someday. I like Jackson, and I know that you like Jackson."

Hayes, who's been strangely silent during this exchange, puts his arm around his younger sister.

"We won't be moving to California, sweetheart."

"Yeah, because your beloved Jackson is in jail." Andrew guffaws at his own words, apparently not caring what he's just done to his daughter. Audrey's hopeful expression falls.

"Is that true, Mom? Why is Jackson in jail? Did he hurt you?"

I pull Audrey to me now and wrap my arms around her.

"No, pumpkin. Jackson would never hurt me. The policemen just wanted to ask him some questions."

"Now they have some questions for you and Andrew."

Audrey and I both start. We turn to see Jackson coming around the corner of the house. Audrey pulls away from me and runs to him. Even with everything going on, part of me melts at the sight of them hugging. Any lingering doubts I had about Jackson's character melt away as well. Jackson towers over Audrey, but with all his muscles and hardness, he can somehow be amazingly gentle with her. He certainly showed me his gentle side last night.

"I knew you couldn't be in jail."

Audrey hugs him again. Jackson's eyes find mine.

"They didn't keep me. They just had some questions. I had nothing to do with this, Emmy."

*I know.* Tears rush to my eyes as I move into the warmth of Jackson's arms. Audrey steps to the side and smiles from ear to ear as Jackson holds me.

"I'm so sorry that I didn't believe you right away."

"I would never hurt you." He whispers in my ear those same words that I just professed to Audrey. My heart just about melts right then and there.

"I heard that one of your friends was behind the robbery? Isn't that too much of a coincidence?" Andrew asks, his tone incredulous.

Fortunately Detective Marshall saves me from answering. "Maybe not a coincidence per se, we are looking into it, of course. But, all indications so far are that Mr. Jackson had nothing to do with the robbery. We do have a few questions for you and Ms. Bennett."

\*\*\*

We parade two doors down to Anne's house. Rather than walk around to the front of the house and down the street, we walk through the backyard of our next-door neighbors, the Millers. They are used to us cutting through their yard, and they don't mind, but thank goodness they both work and are not home to witness it this time. Anne answers the knock at her back door and invites us all inside. The cool kitchen is very welcoming. The sun is quite high in the sky now, and I didn't realize how hot I was sitting out there on my deck.

"Would it be okay if we borrow your kitchen or living room for a little while? The police have a few questions for us, and we can't use our house."

"Of course, of course." Anne gestures for everyone to sit at her kitchen table and begins pouring coffee.

"Be right back," I announce to the group before pulling Jackson back onto Anne's patio. The back of Anne's house is closer to the ground level, so instead of a wooden deck like we have, she has a beautiful stone patio. I close the door for a moment of privacy.

Jackson's blue eyes study me, showing very similar concern as the first time I looked into them. Then he was worried because I'd just fainted. Now, I can imagine he's worried about many things.

"I know that it looks bad, but I swear that I had nothing to do with any of this."

"I really didn't want to think you did, but that photo of you with *him*. And he's your friend."

"The police believe me."

"I believe you, too. I'm sorry that I doubted you at all. I just…"

*Just what?* There are so many things I need to say to him, but the words can't seem to get past the lump in my throat. Jackson's arms move around me. His lips find mine. We share our relief in a perfect kiss.

"Come with me to San Diego. Hayes and Audrey are strong kids. They'll adjust. We'll have a good life there."

"I can't. It's part of the divorce agreement. The kids have to stay here in Williamsburg, and I can't leave them."

"Ask him." Jackson's eyes beg me.

"There's no point. Andrew just made his opinion on the subject very clear."

"Maybe I can talk to him."

"This isn't going to work." My eyes are wet. I look away from Jackson and see Detective Patterson watching us through the window. I clear my throat and step back. Jackson looks up to see her as well.

"Let me take Hayes and Audrey out for a while so that you and Andrew can talk with the police. Would that be okay?"

I nod, knowing that if I speak right now, tears will flow.

## Chapter Thirty-Seven

### Jackson

"Mom isn't going to like this." Audrey hits Hayes on the arm and glares at him to keep quiet. "She's not."

They both look at me.

"I know, but she'll be mad at me, not you. Hopefully I can convince her that I'm doing this for her own good."

Changing the locks didn't work. Emmy refused to get an alarm system. So, we're going with a different tactic—canine threat detection.

I hold the door open for Hayes and Audrey to enter the animal control building. I didn't tell them where we were headed. I just looked up the address on my phone, figured out the directions, and drove here. Hayes's *Mom isn't going to like this* comment were the first words he'd uttered during the entire drive here. Audrey, on the other hand, has talked incessantly. She began the trip by asking several questions, all of which I couldn't answer fully. She finally decided to give up her interrogation and tell me all about some boy band that she's in love with. I didn't need to hear about them, but it was nice to have her chatter to fill the chasm of silence that would have otherwise been there.

"Hello there. How can I help you?"

The woman greets us cheerfully. I'd put her in her fifties, her salt and pepper hair the biggest giveaway. She smiles and walks around the counter to stand nearby. Her happy demeanor does a nice job of cheering up this otherwise drab entryway. It doesn't do much for the smell though—that hits you as soon as you open the front door. It isn't as bad as it could be, but it's dog for sure.

"We'd like to adopt a dog,"

Audrey's face beams. Hayes's expression is guarded, still clearly concerned about his mom's reaction to my plan. No need for him to be worried. I'll be the one taking the full wrath for this one.

"I can help you. I'm April." Her smile grows even larger. "Did you have a breed in mind?"

"Not in particular. We would like something big, but it also has to be family-friendly."

"We have a few dogs here that might be just what you're looking for."

She opens a door and guides us into a room of small kennels. Upon seeing us, the barking escalates to an almost ear-bleeding level. Audrey runs to the closest cage and lets a small black dog lick her hand. She turns to Hayes and smiles. Hayes gives her a tentative smile in return.

"Here we have a yellow lab named Sammy." April gestures to a very large lab. "Sammy's seven. She's very sweet."

Sammy does look very sweet, no doubt about that. Hayes gives her head a pat. Sammy pushes against the front of the kennel for more attention. Hayes smiles fully now.

"Sammy seems like a very sweet dog, but do you have any dogs that meet our criteria that are younger?"

Hayes's smile fades at my words. He likes Sammy, and why not? She's a sweetie, but seven is kind of up there in dog years. I don't want to get them a dog that might not be around too much longer. I'd rather get them one that has almost its whole life ahead of it. I just hope I can get out of here without having to explain that out loud. April gives me a knowing look and walks a little farther down the line. I follow her, but Hayes and Audrey stay with Sammy.

"How about Lucy?"

April gestures towards another kennel. Large brown eyes look back at me. They somehow project sweet, smart, and mischievous all at the same time Those eyes are attached to a Doberman puppy. She's not a tiny puppy, but definitely still young.

"We think she's around four months old."

Audrey catches up to us and squeals with delight. Lucy wags her tail, pushing her nose against the crate.

"Why don't we take her out for a spin?"

Audrey stands aside to make room for April to open the gate. Audrey and Lucy are both practically vibrating with excitement. Hayes walks towards us, too. Lucy's paws hit the floor at a run and she's off— straight toward Hayes. The other dogs bark even louder with the excitement that one of their own is out and running around the room. Audrey chases after Lucy. She and Hayes kneel on the floor as Lucy takes turns licking both their faces. Hayes turns to me, a huge smile on his face. Lucy's the one.

April knows, too. "Why don't you take her home for a trial?" I follow April back to the front desk to begin the paperwork.

## Chapter Thirty-Eight

*Emmy*

"How *do* you explain that, Andrew?"

"I have no idea. I told you. Hayes went into the guest room as soon as he got to our house. He stayed there until dinner, which we had to drag him out to eat. Afterwards, he went back to the guest room until it was time to go to swim practice this morning. I dropped him off at practice. Carson drove the girls in a bit later, at the start of their practice. I never saw Hayes's house key, and I never went in his backpack. I didn't even know that Hayes *had* a house key."

"You knew that we changed the locks. You saw them when you were at our house yesterday."

"Sure, I saw them. That doesn't mean I knew that

you gave Hayes a new key. He usually comes and goes through the garage. Why would I think things would suddenly change? I didn't give it any thought."

What Andrew is saying makes sense, but he had access to the key. He could have made a copy. Maybe he snuck in while Hayes was eating dinner.

"What about your wife?" Detective Marshall asks. "Did she go into Hayes's bedroom?"

"No." Andrew wiggles uncomfortably in his seat. "They don't get along. Hayes hasn't yet accepted Carson; he still views her as the wicked step monster. She's been nothing but wonderful to him, but Hayes doesn't seem to see it that way."

*Oh, Hayes.* Part of me is happy to hear that Hayes is smart enough to avoid Carson, but the other part of me is sad for him. I had no idea that Hayes locks himself away when he's at Andrew's house. It's true that Hayes usually gives vague answers about what they do there, but I thought that was because he didn't want to hurt my feelings by telling me about spending time with Carson. That's why I didn't push him for more information. I didn't want to put him in the middle.

"What about Audrey? Did she have a key as well?" Detective Marshall asks, breaking me out of my Hayes trance.

"No. Just Hayes"

"What did Audrey do at your house?" the detective asks Andrew.

"She and Isabella play together most of the time.

Audrey isn't as difficult."

Anger churns in the pit of my stomach.

"Audrey tries to make everyone happy. She wants to please people, so if you tell her to play with Isabella, then she will."

Andrew's eyes flash their annoyance, and then it's gone. Sometimes I wonder how I never saw this side of Andrew when we were dating. *I was so blind.*

"Where is Mrs. Bennett right now?"

"She's at the pool with Isabella."

"Please call or text her and ask her to come here immediately."

Andrew scoots back suddenly in his chair.

"Is that really necessary?"

Detective Marshall's eyes narrow. "Yes, it's very necessary that we speak with Mrs. Bennett. If you'd like, we can send uniformed officers to pick her up from the pool and take her down to the station for questioning. Is that what you'd prefer?"

"No. That isn't necessary." Andrew's mouth forms a thin line. "Carson has nothing to do with any of this."

Andrew removes his phone from his pocket and begins pecking on the screen.

"Detective Patterson will watch you text your message. Then, please put your phone in the middle of the table." Detective Patterson stands behind Andrew for a moment, nods her head towards Detective Marshall, and then takes her original seat as Andrew slides his phone towards the center of the table.

What in the world will Carson be thinking when she gets the message? Something like *Come to Anne Strickland's house.* Is she with her usual gaggle of pool rats? Did she share the text with them and try to analyze it, or will she keep it hidden and sneak away without revealing that the police want to ask her questions? One thing is for sure. She's blaming me for putting her in this situation.

\*\*\*

Carson arrives within minutes. I don't know the contents of the message that was sent, but it must have communicated urgency. Anne shows Carson to the kitchen and offers her a drink. She's a wonderful hostess who shows no sign of her dislike for Carson, but we share a look that says enough.

Carson is wearing a long, flowing cover-up, the sheer-white material hides nothing. Her bright floral string bikini shines right through the fabric along with her deeply tanned skin. She carries a designer pool bag and wears designer sunglasses that probably cost more than my first car. These things are what really bother me. *Crap*, I have the designer clothes and the glasses—all of it. I struggled with these material things off and on for my whole marriage—wanting to feel worthy of them, but flabbergasted at the prices and the stress that came with owning things that cost that much money.

Those things are very important to Andrew, so he would make sure that Carson has them, just like he made sure that I had them. It's Carson's attitude that bothers me more than anything. She hates me. I hate her. It really boils down to just that. I just wish that I looked better this morning. I'm still wearing the floral dress that I wore to dinner last night. Of course, I didn't *wear* it all night. And I did shower this morning before I came home—with Jackson. My mouth goes dry. At least I had sex with a wonderfully hot man last night, and Carson had Andrew—I win. No comparison there.

"Ms. Bennett, would you and Mr. Bennett please wait outside for a few moments so that we can speak with Mrs. Bennett alone?"

I push my chair back from the table. "Sure." I give Carson a wry smile and walk out the back door with my head held high. Andrew follows.

The sun is way up in the sky, and it's now officially hot. I take a seat under the shade of Anne's patio umbrella. Andrew joins me, but neither of us says a word as we're both seemingly lost in thought.

Carson was very unhappy that I kept the name Bennett when Andrew and I divorced. Some people say that I kept it for the prestige it carries. That's not even remotely true. I kept it only because it's the last name of my children. They have enough to explain to people. I didn't want them to have to explain why their mother's last name is different from theirs. It's as simple as that. I would be proud to go back to my maiden name, Swanson. It's not flashy, but my father was very well respected for his character. Funny how that works. Andrew is respected, but only because of the power his family wields. His character sucks.

The sound of the door opening snaps me out of my thoughts. Anne joins us.

"Why don't you and the kids stay here with us until you get things cleaned up over there? This way you'll be close by."

"Maybe. I don't want to impose."

"Why don't you stay with us?" We all turn to see Vanessa walking towards us. "One of the policemen told me that you were over here. I hope it's okay that I came by."

Vanessa's eyes radiate their usual confidence. As much as I hate to admit it, I probably owe her an apology for the way I acted this morning. I hate it that she was intruding in my life and investigating Jackson, but she only did it because she cares about me. Plus, the information that she presented was truthful. The detectives told me the same thing only minutes later.

It's very sweet of her to offer, but I don't want to stay with her and Andrew. It would be too uncomfortable. I try to school my expression though, since I don't want my feelings to be that obvious.

"You wouldn't be any trouble," she adds with a tentative smile. "The house is large enough for all of us."

Vanessa steps onto the patio. I stand and walk towards her to say hello. She pulls me to her in a tight hug—a real embrace this time.

"Wait, I have an even better idea." She pulls back and looks at me. Her blue eyes flash with excitement. "You can stay at the beach house."

Their beach house is a very large *cottage*—at least that's what they call it, even if it's the largest cottage known to man. It's in Sandbridge, which is south of Virginia Beach, far from the crowds of the boardwalk and strip. It's right on the water. Andrew took Hayes and Audrey there last summer with his other family, but I haven't been there for two years.

"My Andrew's work is preventing us from being there this summer. No one is using it. That way, you all can have some relaxation time before you deal with your house here. You can use it for as long as you'd like."

"Mother, you can't be serious. That is so unfair to Carson. It would be like a slap in the face."

"Carson will understand."

*Highly unlikely based on Andrew's reaction.*

"Emmy, Hayes, and Audrey have been through a horrible ordeal. They need to go away and regroup. It makes perfect sense." Andrew says no more, but his look is seething. "I won't take *no* for an answer, Emmy."

"Well, at least we wouldn't be in anyone's way there." *Plus, we can stay in a beach house and make Andrew and Carson angry at the same time. Done!*

"You wouldn't be in anyone's way here."

Anne's eyes clearly show her disappointment.

"What if we stay at the beach house for a few days, until the police release our house? Then, we'll stay with you, Anne, while we clean it up and get it ready to go on the market. Would that be too much of an imposition?"

She smiles "Of course not."

*Good*. Everyone's happy. Vanessa seems thrilled that I'm taking her up on her offer, Anne is happy that we'll be staying with her, and I'm happy because Andrew seems so *unhappy* about the idea.

## Chapter Thirty-Nine

### Jackson

Our first stop was to a pet superstore where we loaded up on everything a dog could possibly need. Leash, collar, food bowls, food, toys, rawhides, plastic poop bags—you name it, we bought it. We even engraved a little, bone-shaped steel dog tag with the name *Lucy* and their phone number. Adopting Lucy was semi-free, but dog ownership is not.

We were a lively bunch going through the store, but the closer we get to their home, the quieter Hayes and Audrey have become. By the time we hit the neighborhood, they're both totally silent, even Audrey. Part of me wants to ask what's wrong, just so I can get them talking. But, there's no point in that—I know exactly what they're worried about. Emmy will not be thrilled that I adopted a dog for her family behind her back. I just pray that she will eventually see the sense of it.

We're a somber group as we walk down the sidewalk towards Anne's house. Audrey holds Lucy's leash as she trots back and forth across the sidewalk, nose to the ground.

"Your mom will love Lucy."

"She will," Audrey says with confidence that is not expressed in her eyes.

"I sure hope so," is all Hayes adds to the conversation. He looks a bit green.

We take a chance and walk around back to Anne's patio. I don't want to traipse through Anne's house with Lucy, and the last time we were here, everyone was in the back of the house in the kitchen anyway. Emmy calls to us as soon as we turn the corner to the back of the house. Hayes and I see her first. There's a whole crowd out here—Emmy, Anne, Andrew, and Vanessa. They are Emmy's ex-family, and yet they seem to be here all the time.

I turn to look at Audrey who is just behind us. She takes a deep breath and makes the turn around the house with Lucy. Audrey leads Lucy over to her mother. Lucy's head lifts, she sees the new people sitting on the patio, and begins pulling her leash in their direction. Audrey could hold Lucy back, but she doesn't. She lets Lucy pull her and goes along for the ride.

Anne squeals the kind of happy sound that is reserved for puppies and babies. My eyes meet Emmy's.

One look at Emmy, and I know that she knows what I've done.

"What's this?"

Even the tone she uses tells me that she knows exactly what this is—an ambush.

"This is Lucy. Jackson helped us pick her out. Isn't she awesome?"

Audrey's voice cracks with nervousness. Her eyes are pleading. Emmy can't say *no* to her.

Lucy stills for a moment as she looks from Anne to Andrew and then to Emmy. As if knowing which person she has to impress, she noses Emmy's leg. Emmy stares at her and then glares at me. Slowly her glare softens, and she reaches down and scratches Lucy behind the ear.

*Gotcha.*

Lucy smiles a huge doggy smile, sits back on her haunches, and then plops her front paws in Emmy's lap. Emmy lets out a giggle, and I can literally hear Hayes's exhale. He smiles a small smile of relief.

"Why is Lucy here?"

Even though Emmy clearly knows, she wants me to squirm.

My turn to speak up. "In addition to being a great companion for your children, Lucy is going to be your home alarm. You said that you couldn't afford an alarm system. Well, Lucy will do the job."

"Is she dangerous?"

We all look at Lucy, who is now trying to launch her whole body into Emmy's lap. Lucy's mouth is open, her tongue lolling out to the side. My eyebrows raise. Do I really have to answer that question?

"Fine. She isn't dangerous."

"Definitely not, but when she gets bigger, she'll be intimidating to people who don't know her. That can't hurt."

Hayes and Audrey kneel in front of their mom. They rub Lucy and let her lick them, even in the face. Emmy lets out a huge sigh.

Andrew, who has been silently taking in the scene, grimaces.

"Do not let that filthy dog lick you in the face." The kids don't listen. If anything, they lean in for more.

Emmy removes Lucy's paws from her lap and slowly stands.

"Jackson, may I talk with you privately?"

*Crap.* Here it comes.

***

We walk back over to Emmy's yard and then onto her deck. Neither of us speak on the way. It feels like I'm being sent to the principal's office, or worse. Maybe Emmy's trying to figure out what to say and how to say it. I don't know. I don't like it, but then I knew when I adopted Lucy that Emmy would be pissed.

We step onto her deck and into a shady spot in the corner. Neither of us sit. Instead, we lean against the railing. Emmy is still quiet, her eyes focused away from me. I finally give in and speak.

"It isn't a done deal, just a trial period."

"What?"

"Lucy. She isn't officially adopted. It's kind of a rent-to-own kind of deal. If you don't like her, we can take her back."

"I can't take Lucy back. You see how Hayes and Audrey look at Lucy. They're already totally in love with her. The last thing I can handle right now is a dog, but I now have one. Why didn't you ask me first?"

"I think that's obvious."

Her eyes meet mine now, chestnut brown with bright spots of anger. Apparently she's going to make me say it.

"If I had asked you about getting a dog, what would you have said?"

"I would have said *no*. I can't handle taking care of a dog on top of everything else going on."

"And that's why I didn't ask you. She'll be good for you and for your children. She's a sweet dog, and Dobermans are a very smart breed. She's perfect."

"There you go again, telling me what I need to do. I don't need you telling me what to do every five seconds. We were doing just fine before you came here and showed me how *unsafe* our lives were. Look what a mess things are now!"

*Can they hear us from Anne's house?*

"You aren't suggesting that I had anything to do with your current predicament, are you? You said you believe me. The police let me go. I didn't rob you, Emmy. I didn't hold you at gunpoint. All I did was try to keep you safe. That's all I thought about with the dog. I just want you and your family to be safe."

"You just saddled me with something else to take care of when I'm still reeling from being robbed."

"Bullshit. I know that you're upset about the robbery, but there's something else going on here. Why don't you admit what it is that really has you upset?"

Emmy's fuming mad now. Her cheeks and neck are red and splotchy. Somehow I'm keeping my cool.

"You're in love with me, Emmy." She immediately begins shaking her head. "You are, and you know what? I'm in love with you, too."

I hadn't yet pictured how I would tell Emmy that I love her, but I wouldn't have dreamed it would be this way.

"No. You need to leave now. Go to San Diego where you belong. You were supposed to leave days ago. You were supposed to leave this morning."

"We deserve a chance to figure this out."

"There is no chance for us. I told you. I'm not

holding you back. No more regrets."

"It's more than that, isn't it? Maybe you're afraid that you'll regret your decision to be with me, just like you regret being with Andrew. Life is full of chances, and that's a chance worth taking. Can't you see that, Emmy? To hell with your *no more regrets* mantra. I'll stay here with you. This is where I want to be. Sure, there's a chance of failure and regret, but there's also the chance that we'll both be very happy. You can't be happy without taking some risk."

"You have to leave."

Emmy's stiff jaw makes her entire face stern. She looks away and then her whole body follows.

*I'm losing her!*

"I'm not allowed to leave town. I have to stay until the police tell me that I can go. Let's use this time to be together and get to know each other."

"Stay if you have to stay, but I don't want to see you anymore."

She turns and walks away from me, leaving me alone with my very unmanly tears.

# Chapter Forty

## *Emmy*

The Bennett beach house is just how I remember it. That isn't a surprise since it's only been a couple years since I've been here. Somehow it seems *much* longer than that. Last time I was here, I was married to Andrew. We were a family. This isn't a place that's filled with happy memories though. This is where Andrew and I visited when we told his parents that we were officially engaged. They were so angry. I wanted them to love me so badly back then. I wanted to prove to them that I could be a good wife to Andrew and that I could fit into their world.

They were correct all along. Maybe not for the right reasons, but Andrew and I weren't made for each other, not for the long haul. The only good things that came from our marriage are Hayes and Audrey. They are worth fifteen years of marriage to the wrong man. And Vanessa isn't so bad now. She's been wonderful lately—especially in the past few days—and now she's letting us stay here. This family time is just what we need to recharge and process everything that's happened. Plus, I have a ton of schoolwork to catch up on. I will be lucky if I pass this last class, even with such a great excuse.

Luckily, the police let us come here. We aren't far from home, but we are out of town. Detective Marshall wouldn't let Andrew or Jackson leave town at all.

*Jackson*.

I was so rude to him; I totally crushed him. He isn't responsible for what happened to us. I know that he isn't, but I needed some excuse to get away. Childish, but I couldn't handle the emotions coursing through me anymore. Jackson was right to say I'm scared, but I'm not scared of loving him. *I do love him*. But, he needs to live his life. He belongs in California, not in Virginia with a semi-crazy woman and her two children. I can't live with the fear that he might regret not following his plan. He might be upset now, but in time, he will see that I'm right. He'll get over me and start a new life. I will be here, like always, but now constantly reminded of Jackson every time I look at Lucy.

She's snoozing soundly on the couch between

Hayes and Audrey. She's a sweet dog, and she loves the beach.

We left to come here within thirty minutes of my conversation with Jackson. Detective Patterson escorted me into my house and watched as I threw a few items of clothing into a large suitcase. I barely even know what I packed. I just picked a few things off the floor of my bedroom. Fortunately, the criminals didn't do any damage to my van. I didn't think about that until just before I finished packing. It was a huge relief to open the door and see the garage looking like it always does. Sure, it's messy, but it's comfortable messy. It's our messy and not the disaster of the rest of the house.

I don't know when Jackson drove away, but his truck was nowhere to be seen when we left for the beach. He won't know where we went, but it's better that way—a clean break and all. Jackson does have my cell phone number. Maybe it doesn't matter though because he hasn't called. I've kept my phone close by in case the police call. Deep down I want to know if Jackson calls, too, but I haven't made up my mind if I'm going to answer that call or not. Probably not.

We may not be staying here for too long anyway. I thought it would be good to get away, but it's hard to think about anything other than Jackson and our destroyed home. The kids were thrilled when we first arrived. They ran on the beach and played in the surf with Lucy for a few hours before they plopped on the couch, all of them exhausted.

Their happiness quickly turned to horror when they remembered how bad the cell service is here and that there is no WIFI. No WIFI, the nightmare realization for a teenager. Their texts aren't going through, and the web is super-slow. We make the most of it for now. They cuddle up on the sofa with a mostly dried-off Lucy to watch a movie.

Maybe I'm getting calls from the police and Jackson, but they aren't getting through? It's strange that Hope and Anne haven't tried to contact me either. I dial Anne's number, and nothing happens. I try Hope's with the same result. Next, I text both of them to tell them that we're here and doing okay. It looks like the texts go through, but neither answer. Under the circumstances, they have to be keeping their phones handy. I finally admit defeat and lay my phone on the coffee table.

What if Jackson is trying to contact me and he can't get through? He'll be so worried. A sharp pain emanates from my lip, and I realize that I'm chewing on it. *Stop doing this to yourself.* Jackson might just think that I don't want to talk to him, and I don't, so it's best that any calls he *might* be making don't come through. It's pretty obvious that I would answer them. Big sigh. I need to stick to my guns and stay away from Jackson.

A knock at the door brings me out of my thoughts.

*Did Jackson find us?* My face immediately flushes

at the possibility that Jackson could be waiting behind the front door. Another big sigh. *That isn't supposed to be my first reaction.* I'm really not good at this sticking to my guns thing.

"Who is it?" Hayes questions.

"I don't know, honey. I'll go see."

My legs are like jelly as I walk to the door, every step bringing more hope that it is indeed Jackson. My trembling fingers turn the doorknob.

Vanessa.

Not Jackson.

A whoosh escapes my lips. I quickly make my mouth form a smile and try to look happy at the sight of my ex-mother-in-law standing before me. It's not her fault that she isn't Jackson, and it was thoughtful of her to knock. This is her house, and she's definitely under no obligation to do so.

"I'm sorry to intrude on your family time with Audrey and Hayes. It's just that I couldn't get you all off my mind. I've been worried sick. Would you mind terribly if I stay here with you tonight?"

In rare Vanessa form, she looks distraught. There are dark half-moons under her eyes. Not only are they not covered with concealer, her make-up looks less than perfect, and her Bermuda shorts are wrinkled from the trip here. I don't want anyone to worry about us, but it's nice that she cares enough to make the drive here to be with us. I longed for her acceptance for years, and her efforts over the last few days show that she thinks of me as family now.

Funny that it took a divorce for that to happen, but whatever the reason, she's here, and I'm grateful.

"Of course. It's so nice of you to come."

Whether it's from Vanessa's kindness or the fact that it isn't Jackson standing here in front of me, my eyes are now wet with tears. Vanessa's become wet as well as she pulls me to her for another tight, warm embrace.

## Chapter Forty-One

### Jackson

My first stop after leaving Emmy was at a bar near my hotel—I thought that it would help to drown my sorrows in some kind of microbrew. If that doesn't work, there's always Scotch. I have nothing better to do while I wait for the police to give me the go ahead to leave town, right? *Wrong*. One beer tells me that this isn't the place for me. I'm too antsy. I need to be doing something.

Emmy didn't mean what she said. I know that. She's afraid—afraid of being hurt and afraid of making me regret staying with her. *Not gonna happen*. Sure Marco's been waiting for me out in San Diego, but he will understand. Maybe he'll want to move back to the East Coast and start our business here. I'm the one who wanted it to be in San Diego. Now, I want to be here. I'm not ready to give up on Emmy, and I won't let her give up on me. We have to at least give this a shot to see where it leads.

There's so much about this case that bothers me, but the only thing that I can do for myself is to figure out how the hell Smitty figures into this. Was this whole scam all his doing? Was he hired by someone else? Smitty is my responsibility. If I hadn't gotten him off the hook for the Norfolk robbery, then he would likely be in prison right now and would never have been able to rob Emmy in the first place. And what about his wife, Candy? How does she fit into all of this?

*** 

Smitty's home address is buried in a book somewhere in my personal effects, which are on their way to California. A quick call to a mutual buddy gets me Smitty's address. I find it easily using the GPS on my phone—wonderful invention. Smitty lives only a couple miles from Emmy's house. The neighborhood is respectable and well-maintained. It's nowhere as nice as Emmy's, but most aren't. I park in their driveway behind Candy's Toyota coupe. It's the same car she was driving when I last saw her.

The talk show playing on the television many decibels louder than it should be gives away the fact that she's home. So, I keep knocking. Candy wrenches the door open after the third knock.

"You!" Her brow furrows. "What the hell do you want?"

Her words come out as snarls. The tone matches the look she's sporting today: large, fluffy, pink robe and flannel pajamas, even as hot as it is outside. She carries a bottle of bourbon in the crook of her arm. This is not her usual look. Candy is around 5'7" with an athletic build. I've rarely seen her in sweatpants or yoga pants, and never in pajamas. She has greenish-brown eyes and cherry red hair that she keeps cut short. Today, it's far from styled. Several pieces are out of place.

"Can I talk to you about what's been going on?" She sighs an extra long sigh and holds the door open for me to enter. I step directly into the living room with the large, loud television. I pick up the remote control off the coffee table and turn the volume down to a reasonable level. Candy resumes her spot on the left-hand side of the couch. This is obviously her spot because of the glass within arm's reach and the number of used tissues that lie on the floor at her feet. She continues to hug the bottle of bourbon.

Candy takes a drink from her glass, replaces it on the coaster, and stares straight ahead at the television.

"Do you know where he is?"

"No idea. That's what I told the police when they came by."

I take a seat next to her on the couch, but not too close. It's probably best if I keep my distance right now.

"Did you know?"

She turns and looks at me now, her eyes wet with tears.

"Did I know what? That my husband was involved in a robbery? No idea. I've been so worried about him since Tuesday morning. I thought that he was at work Monday night. He even texted me a couple times, just like he always does. I usually see him in the mornings before I go to work, but he didn't come home. He told me that he went out to breakfast with a coworker. No biggie, at least I didn't think so. I left him alone during the day so he could rest. That's the schedule every day."

She grabs another tissue from the box and dabs her eyes. I want to ask questions, but she's on a roll, so I just let her continue.

"He wasn't here when I came home Tuesday. I've called and texted, and I haven't heard from him at all, not a word since he told me he was going out to breakfast."

She's crying in earnest now. I tentatively place my hand on her shoulder.

"I was afraid he was having an affair. I've been home crying about that since Tuesday. Then the police came this morning, asking questions about a robbery. *I want to kill him*. We were doing so well. I thought we'd recovered nicely from the mess he got himself into the last time. He's been seeing a counselor. I never suspected a thing."

I hug Candy to me now and let her sob into my shoulder. The wetness of her tears seeps through my t-shirt, but I just let her cry it out.

"Get away from my wife." Smitty stands at the edge of the hallway with a gun.

*I did not see that coming.* Apparently Candy didn't expect this either, because her mouth opens in shock.

I scoot back from Candy and turn to face Smitty.

"Candy was upset about you leaving. I was just trying to console her."

Smitty shakes his head, causing his blond hair to move with him. It's a strange sight since until Monday, I'd never seen him with anything other than a crew cut. His blue eyes radiate a level of pure anger that I've never seen on Smitty before. He used to be such a laid back guy.

"What happened to you, man?"

He takes two steps closer and raises his Smith and Wesson a few inches higher in the air so that it's more level with my head than my chest. I stand, and he raises the gun higher to match my movement.

*Options?*

Not many. Smitty's leg isn't as strong as it was before he was shot, but his aim is still dead on. And the coffee table sits between us. He would easily be able to take me down before I reach him.

"Don't even try it, old man." A wicked smile forms

on his lips. "Why couldn't you just stay out of the fucking way? Always on my back about every fucking thing. What are the chances that she would be late? You were supposed to be my alibi, you asshole. Instead, you end up being the fucking savior of the day...again. Can't you ever just mind your own business?"

Despite Smitty's anger, his shooting hand is calm and still. Candy's shaking like a leaf. She pushes the bourbon bottle to the side and stands on unsteady legs. With tears still streaming down her face, she takes a step forward.

"Candy, stay out of this," Smitty sneers. "This is between me and Mr. Good Samaritan here."

"No, you can't shoot him. That's Jackson. Put the gun down, honey."

Smitty doesn't take his eyes off of me.

"Sit down, Candy."

She stops her forward movement but stands in the same spot, about four feet from him.

*Focus on the situation at hand.*

"Why did you do it?"

"I wanted a better life for Candy and me. I don't make shit at the university. I was going to get a huge payoff when the job was over. Instead, you got involved, and those stupid thugs I hired ratted me out."

"Someone hired you to rob Emmy?"

"Nice try, man. I'm not telling you anything."

Candy's crying becomes louder and is now

composed mostly of grunts and heavy breathing. She's angry. Her hands form into tight fists. "How could you do this to us?"

Smitty's eyes twitch. He holds his gaze on me, but he's dying to look at Candy. She takes one step closer. She's only a few feet away now. I take a large step to the side in Candy's general direction, but most importantly, I side-step the coffee table. Smitty keeps his eyes locked on mine, but I'm close enough to Candy now that he can see her in his peripheral vision. She takes another step closer and squeezes his left arm. His right arm keeps the gun trained on me.

"Please, honey. Put the gun down. You can't shoot Jackson."

"I absolutely can."

My gut tells me that he wouldn't shoot me, but Smitty's hard eyes tell me that he wouldn't hesitate.

Candy lightly caresses Smitty's cheek. He looks at her, and that's when I make my move. I leap across the room, closing the space between us and tackling Smitty to the ground. Candy falls with us, caught in the scramble for the gun.

The gun fires.

Candy shrieks.

Smitty freezes.

My hand finds the gun, and I turn it toward him. He pays no attention to me. All his focus is on Candy as blood soaks her pink fuzzy robe.

The wound is low, looks to be in her right thigh.

T*he same place where Smitty was shot*. Smitty pulls off his t-shirt and ties it around her leg as a tourniquet. I reach for my phone and dial 9-1-1. It's surreal that I'm speaking with an emergency operator again. I just did this when Emmy fainted.

I impart the urgency of the situation to the operator, and once I'm assured that an ambulance is on its way, I ask her to send a policeman and alert Detectives Marshall and Patterson as well. I'm not getting Smitty out of this one. I sit with him and Candy while we wait for the ambulance. The make-shift tourniquet seems to be doing its job. Candy is weak, but still conscious when the police arrive. Fortunately, they recognize Smitty as someone they've been searching for.

I readily surrender Smitty's pistol and keep my hands up. I didn't speak with him, but I recognize one of the officers from Emmy's house this morning. Maybe that will keep me from being arrested before the detectives arrive.

Smitty kisses Candy on the forehead, tells her that he loves her, and goes easily with the policemen. He knows that the ambulance is waiting down the block until the police have cleared any threats. He doesn't want to delay Candy's treatment any longer than necessary. He doesn't even look at me as he's handcuffed and escorted outside.

I take his place at Candy's side and hold her hand until the EMTs hover around her.

Detective Marshall is smiling when he and

Detective Patterson enter the house.

"It's not over. Smitty was hired to do this job. There's someone else out there."

\*\*\*

Do I call Emmy now, or do I let her cool off first? She needs to know what happened, but what if she won't talk to me? It would be much better to speak with her about this in person. Maybe then I could talk some sense into her. But—and this is a big but— I have no idea where she is. Maybe Anne would tell me where she went. Maybe Carter? But it's already after nine-o'clock. Showing up unannounced would not get me on their good side. Maybe a phone call would be okay? It's not that late.

I trudge into the entry of my hotel and stop in my tracks.

Marci, the woman from the pool the other night that Emmy can't stand, is here, sitting in the lobby. She lifts her head at the sound of the automatic glass door, and there it is. *Busted*. I walk toward her as she stands to greet me. She's wearing a knock-out of a dress—red, cut low, hem high, made to look even higher by her three-inch heels. Her bleach blond hair is down, large dangly hoops fall from her ears. She smiles a wicked smile, places her hands on my shoulders, and then pulls me in for a hello hug. I pull back quickly.

"What are you doing here?"

"I heard that Emmy went out of town, and she left you here all alone." She makes a tsk-tsk sound with her red, pouty lips as she runs a finger down my chest, following it with her eyes. "I don't want you to be lonely."

"How did you know where to find me?"

There are tons of hotels in this area, and we definitely did not talk about the subject.

"A friend told me. That's supposed to be a secret. She wanted you to think that I followed you here, but that sounds so desperate. I am anything but desperate."

*Huh?*

"What friend?"

Have I told anyone where I'm staying? No. Only Emmy knows.

"That isn't important."

I grab her wrist and remove her hand from my chest.

"It is *very* important. Who is it?"

The urgency in my voice must get her attention, because she snaps her head back and looks into my eyes.

"The person did me a favor by telling me where you're staying, and I did a favor for them. There's nothing wrong with that."

"The police might beg to differ. *Who is the friend?*"

The mention of the police has the desired effect. Marci's eyes widen. "It's nothing criminal."

"Who is it?"

She sighs. "Vanessa Bennett."

"Vanessa?" That is a surprise. "Wait a minute. What favor did you do for her?"

"I told her that I wouldn't tell anyone that I saw her at the hardware store yesterday. It's silly, really."

Marci keeps talking, but her words are now unclear as the realization dawns on me. *Vanessa.*

"Was Vanessa looking at locks or keys?"

"How did you know that?"

"Why don't you have a seat? You're going to be talking to the police after all."

I find Detective Marshall's number on my recent calls and push the send button. My knees are so weak, I lean on a nearby chair for support. Marci plops down in it and places her hand on my thigh. *This woman is incorrigable.* The call connects.

"It was Vanessa Bennett. I have a witness at my hotel with me now who saw her in the lock section of the hardware store. She was also in Emmy's kitchen yesterday when she brought lunch to us. She could have easily seen the lock code printed on the package and bought another lock set with that same code. That would give her keys that fit Emmy's doors. It all makes sense."

"Slow down," Detective Marshall demands. "You're saying it's the mother-in-law?"

"Yes! Get to her house. Where is Emmy and her family?"

"Shit. They're at the in-laws' beach house."

"What? No! Where the hell are they?"

"Sandbridge. I'll call the local police now and get a car over there. I'll have someone call you back with the address. Patterson and I will get over to the Bennett house right now."

I push *end* and immediately call Emmy's phone. It goes straight to voicemail. *Shit.*

"Stay put. The police will be here soon." I yell at Marci as I'm already running back out the door.

Fortunately, my hotel is near the interstate. I don't have the address yet, but Sandbridge is easily an hour and a half away. *Not that I'll be obeying speed limits to get there.* Sandbridge is just south of Virginia Beach and not far from the base where I was stationed.

I floor my truck and merge into traffic, heading even farther away from California. A small smile forms on my lips. This trip is like a parallel to my life. If the opposite of California is what will make me happy, then that's where I'll be. I have some say in this, too. Emmy can't make me go if I don't want to. Now, if I can just get Emmy on the phone. This time it just rings. This is going to be a long trip.

## Chapter Forty-Two

### Emmy

Both Hayes and Audrey are fast asleep on the couch when the movie ends. I nodded off a few times myself. I stand and walk to the large window overlooking the water. In true beach fashion, the first level of the house consists of the garage and storage. The best views are from the second and third stories anyway.

The second level is the living space, which consists of one large living area, a kitchen, and a recreation room. There are three couches here, but my children and Lucy are all cuddled up on one. Hayes and Audrey will likely sleep there all night, but I need to get Lucy outside for a potty break before I lay down myself. I can't trust her to make it through the night without an accident.

Before waking Lucy, I step outside onto the patio to tell Vanessa that I'll be going outside for a few minutes. I don't want her to worry that I'm not here, or become frightened when she sees a dark figure out on the beach. I find Vanessa lying in one of the chairs looking out at sea.

"Beautiful night."

I give Vanessa a quick smile and take a moment to appreciate the view. It is gorgeous. Vast, dark, gray water that meets the dark sky above it. The sound of the surf and touch of salt in the air. There's nothing like the beach.

"I'm going to take Lucy for a walk on the beach."

"Would it be okay if I join you?"

"Sure."

*How great is this?* Vanessa used to hate me. Now she cares enough about us to let us stay in her house, and she actually wants to spend time with me. *I would have killed for this attention fifteen years ago.*

\*\*\*

The warm temperature is buffered by the light breeze coming off the water. The moon is nowhere in sight, tucked behind a cloud, apparently. There are few lights coming from the homes that line the beach. The darkness makes it difficult to make out

Lucy as she runs in and out of the surf. Basically, I'm watching for the black blur that moves around the beach. Vanessa and I stand together and look out into the darkness.

"I'm sorry about your man toy."

"What? Do you mean Jackson?"

What an odd thing to say, and what an odd choice of words coming from Vanessa.

"Yes. Sorry that he's with someone else tonight."

"What do you mean?" *With someone else?* "How do you know that?"

*And why are you telling me?*

"He's with Marci Fernico. She has the hots for him, you know."

"She's made that pretty obvious. What do you mean *with him*?"

My stomach doesn't feel so good.

"A little birdie told me that she was going to meet him at his hotel. I'm sure he said *no* once or twice, but you know Marci, she doesn't stop until she gets what she wants."

I'm pretty sure I have an ulcer now. Can they come on suddenly?

"Why are you telling me this?"

"I wanted to make sure you knew about him and Marci before…"

"Before what?"

"Before you die."

*What?*

I strain my eyes to focus on Vanessa. She's

holding something dark in her hand, and it's pointed at me.

*A gun.*

*Again.*

This time I've made sure that Jackson won't be here to rescue me. And what about Vanessa? She likes me now, right?

*I'm such an idiot.*

"Why are you doing this?"

"You always were a real pain in the ass."

"What are you talking about?"

"I'm the one who stole the Rutledge ring."

My knees wobble, but I hold on and remain standing.

*Vanessa?*

"You were never worthy of it. Carson is the one who should have had it all along. Carson is the woman Andrew should have married from the beginning. I didn't want you to wear it, and I didn't want you to sell it to someone else."

*But she's been so nice to me.*

The truth slams into me in what feels like a physical blow. I grab onto my knees for support and to keep myself upright. Vanessa's recent niceness was all an act to get me to trust her.

"I wouldn't have sold the ring."

"I've had someone watching you for the last few years. When I learned you were selling your other jewelry, I couldn't take the chance that you might sell the ring, too. Such a crass thing to do, selling jewelry on the street corner."

"It wasn't like that. The divorce didn't leave me with enough money to live on. I had to do something."

"You were supposed to leave town."

"How could I leave town? Hayes and Audrey had to stay here in Williamsburg. I wasn't going anywhere without them."

Hayes and Audrey are asleep in the house. Even if they were awake and could make out our figures in the darkness, they'd never be able to tell that Vanessa is holding me at gunpoint. My heart breaks for them. What kind of grandmother does this? Grandmothers are supposed to be warm and make chocolate chip cookies. My mother could have been that kind of grandma, but I never gave her the chance.

What will happen to Hayes and Audrey if Vanessa kills me? They'll be forced to stay with Andrew and Carson.

"You are stubborn. I'll give you that. You've taken all my punches. I'm the one who helped Carson move back to town after her divorce. I knew that she never got over her feelings for Andrew."

*You bitch!*

"You went through the humiliation of the divorce and you stayed. You couldn't afford to stay in your house, and you were still planning to stay in town. I mean, honestly, take a hint already. No one wants you here."

"Am I supposed to just leave Hayes and Audrey here with Andrew and Carson? They don't even like him anymore."

*But they do like Jackson. So do I.*

"Andrew is a good father, and they'll grow to love Carson. Everything will settle down once you're out of the way."

"Vanessa, you don't have to hurt me. You have the ring back now. You don't have to ever see me again."

She takes a step closer to me.

"I want more than that. I thought the ring was what I really wanted, but it isn't enough. I want you out of our lives for good."

She raises the gun. This one is tiny compared to the one that Mr. Lehman—well the guy pretending to be Mr. Lehman—pointed at me. Does she even know how to fire it? Her tight voice tells me that she's going to try. Besides, she wouldn't be telling me all of this if she planned to let me live.

*Do something!*

The sound of a siren cuts through the ocean breeze. Vanessa turns towards her house. The flashing blue lights reflect against the side of the house.

*This is my chance.*

I turn and run for the water. It's the only place I can think of going. There's nowhere on the beach to hide, and running toward a dune in the loose sand would be too slow. She'd shoot me for sure.

Vanessa fires.

*I'm okay.* The bullet didn't hit me.

My progress slows as I hit the water, but I keep moving. *Don't look back. Keep moving forward.*

A bark sounds to my right.

*Lucy!*

She bounds towards me.

*Please don't shoot Lucy.*

Just keep moving.

Another shot.

*My shoulder!*

*I've been hit!*

The pain shoots through my body, taking my breath away. I fall, the surf catching me as a wave rolls over my head. Instinct makes me push upward. I cry out in pain, but my face is out of the water, and I can breathe.

Lucy presses her nose to my cheek. I chance a look back at Vanessa. She's still in the same spot, made easier to see by the white shirt she wears.

"Drop your weapon!"

Two blurry, dark figures move up behind her.

A gun fires.

*There's only darkness.*

## *Chapter Forty-Three*

### *Jackson*

I answer the call on the first ring.

"It's Marshall. Are you driving?"

"Yeah."

*Shit. It's bad news. Why is he asking that?*

I give a hard yank to the steering wheel and move to the shoulder.

"Tell me."

"She's going to be okay."

Relief bursts through my body like fireworks, leaving me lightheaded, but I still don't miss the fact that he said *going to be*.

"What happened?"

The ringing in my ears makes it hard to

concentrate on Detective Marshall's words.

"Vanessa shot her in the shoulder. She's on her way to the hospital now—Sentara Princess Anne."

"In an ambulance or a chopper?"

A few long seconds pass. *Not good. What's he hiding?*

"A chopper." *No!* "But only because Vanessa needs it. She was shot by one of the first responders—in the chest. Vanessa is in critical condition. They're not sure she's going to make it. Emmy's injuries aren't as serious. She'll be okay."

"I'll be there in a few minutes. What about Hayes and Audrey?"

"They're fine. They missed all the action. One of the officers is driving them."

*Have to get to them.*

I floor the gas pedal and merge back into traffic.

"Tell me what happened."

"I don't have many details. Vanessa came to the beach house sometime this evening. The first responders found Emmy and Vanessa on the beach when they arrived. Emmy was in the water and Vanessa was shooting at her and the dog." *Lucy!* "Lucy's fine. Emmy was shot in the shoulder twice. We're en-route ourselves. We'll see you there shortly."

"Thank you for calling me. I'll see you there."

*Emmy was shot.*

*She's in the hospital.*

*I wasn't there for her.*

***

Parking is easy to find this time of night. I sprint to the Emergency entrance. This hospital is huge, and that seems like a good place to start.

The young man behind the desk stands as I run to him. His green eyes study me, anticipating the actions that may be required of him.

"A woman was just brought in by ambulance— Emmy, Emilou Bennet—where is she?"

He moves his computer mouse a few times and clicks.

"Are you family?"

I shake my head. *I wish*.

"Her family is through those doors," he gestures to the glass doors across the room, "to the right and down the hall. Look for signs that say *Surgical Waiting Area*."

"Thank you."

I take off at a run again, bursting through the doors, and sprinting down the empty hallway. The corridor opens up to a large waiting area lined with chairs. Is this it? I stop and take a second to look around. The room is a sea of blues and greens to calm those waiting here—*I am not calm*—and mostly empty. *Where are they?*

"Jackson?"

Hayes and Audrey sit together on a small couch in the corner. Audrey's cheeks and eyes are wet and red from crying. She jumps up and meets me halfway. Her arms move around my neck. She holds me so tightly, as if her life depends on it. I hug her back and lift her up as I walk to Hayes. He stands as well and joins us. My eyes are wet with tears.

"I was so worried about you."

Hayes steps back. His eyes are wet as well, but he's trying to keep it together for Audrey.

"Mom was shot."

My hand finds his shoulder. His normally light brown eyes are heavy with worry, dark circles beneath them. He looks absolutely exhausted.

"Your mom is the strongest woman I know. She's going to be okay."

Someone nearby clears his throat. It's a police officer. He holds out his hand, and I shake it.

"You must be Jackson."

My forehead furrows. *They told him about me?*

"They've been asking for you almost since we arrived at the scene. I'm Officer Dias."

"Thanks for taking care of them."

He nods. Audrey untangles herself from me and drops to the floor. We all squeeze onto the love seat, which means Audrey is practically in my lap, and that's fine. I put my arm around her shoulders and she snuggles closer. *This feels amazing.* Heidi would have been about fourteen now, if she had lived. Not that I deserve it, but I'm not giving this up—Emmy, Hayes, Audrey, and even Lucy. *I will not let Emmy push me away.*

"Where's Lucy?"

"She's with my partner. Quite the hero puppy you've got there."

Hayes smiles a huge smile.

"Lucy helped save Mom."

"What?"

"She did," Officer Dias interjects. "Lucy was holding onto Ms. Bennett's shirt to keep her head out of the water. She was trying her mightiest to pull her to shore."

\*\*\*

Detectives Marshall and Patterson arrive about an hour later. It's been a long hour with only one update on Emmy's condition, and that's because Officer Dias went to ask about her. We all hunker down and wait some more, hopefully only a little longer.

Andrew's eyes are huge when he turns the corner and sees me here. He and an older gentleman, whom I assume is his father, make their way toward us. Both are eyeing me suspiciously. Andrew II looks like a carbon copy of his son with a fit body and the same tan skin. Sure, his silver hair reveals his age, but he looks great, with hardly a wrinkle to be seen. Very impressive for a man who has to be in his sixties. That's the only nice thing that I can say about him. He never accepted Emmy into the family either. *Did he know what his wife planned?*

Hayes and Audrey don't run to their dad. They

don't even stand up. Audrey says a mere *hello*. Hayes barely looks in Andrew's direction as he moves closer to me. Andrew doesn't miss it.

"Any news?"

"Both Ms. Bennett and Mrs. Bennett are still in surgery."

"What is this bullshit that Vanessa is being charged with attempted murder?"

Detective Marshall steps toward the elder Mr. Bennett.

"Your wife tried to kill her ex-daughter-in-law."

"Do you know who you are talking to, detective?"

"Yes, sir, I do. But you need to know that we have witnesses. Officer Dias here is one of them."

*Go detective!* Officer Dias stands and introduces himself.

"My partner and I were first on the scene. I'm sorry to give you the news, Mr. Bennett, but we know what we saw."

"Attempted murder is only one of the charges. She will also be charged with felony theft for starters. There's no telling what else will come up when the DA gets his hands on her."

"This is ridiculous. We will fight these charges."

Detective Marshall does not back down. Instead, he steps closer so that they're only about a foot apart and looks Mr. Bennett right in the eye.

"You go right ahead. You are in for a long road, Mr. Bennett. Both you and your son will also need to be questioned, once your wife comes out of surgery."

Mr. Bennett inhales deeply, his chest protrudes in an almost too grand gesture of superiority. He says nothing else and instead turns, walks away from our group, and sits in a chair on the other side of the waiting room. All eyes now turn to Andrew.

"I guess I deserve this."

He's talking about Hayes and Audrey and their disinterest in him. That's clear from the forlorn look in his eyes.

"I haven't been the best father to you two, and I'm sorry about that."

Audrey stands and hugs him, albeit a bit awkwardly. Hayes makes eye contact with his father—an improvement in his demeanor—but no movement to stand or follow Audrey's lead.

***

We all stand when a doctor walks toward us. He's tall and African American, and that's about all I can tell about him as he's hidden behind his scrubs, cap, and mask. He removes his mask as he approaches our group. *What is he going to say?*

*Please let Emmy be okay.*

My arm is still around Audrey, so I pull her closer to me in anticipation of the news. I think it will be good—based on the surgeon's eyes. He's not wearing the sad face of someone about to give bad news. Hayes is standing close. I put my other arm around his shoulders. I don't pull him into me, but I want to support him as best as I can. He's proven himself to be strong during this, but he's only fifteen. He doesn't have to do this all on his own.

"Are you the family of Emilou Bennett?"

We nod in unison. Detective Marshall is the only one who actually says *yes* out loud as we stare at the doctor waiting for his news.

"Ms. Bennett is in recovery and resting nicely."

Hayes's relief is evident as his body practically falls into mine. I pull him to me. Audrey is crying again. I think I am, too. If not, I will be soon. The relief is huge.

"My team removed two small caliber bullets from her right shoulder area. One bullet tore through only muscle, and the other penetrated her Subscapular Fossa."

*Don't know what that is.* Guess the others in our group don't either based on their confused looks.

"That's one of the bones in the shoulder. The bullet went through cleanly. We were able to repair the area, and it will take some time to heal, but she is going to be just fine."

That's all I need to hear, which is good because the blood rushes from my head. My ears are now ringing too loudly to hear what the doctor is saying. I take a few deep breaths, in and out.

*Concentrate.*

Audrey is hugging my waist now in a fit of full-on sobbing. *The relief is so immense.* I brush her soft hair and kiss the top of her head. My gestures bring even more tears. She looks up to me, and our eyes connect.

"You can't leave us."

"I'm not going to. I'll talk to your mom and make her understand. I'm not going anywhere."

"It's okay with me."

My gaze leaves Audrey and looks at Andrew, who just spoke those words.

"What's okay with you?"

"I will call my lawyer tomorrow. It's okay with me if Hayes and Audrey move away from Williamsburg. I haven't been the best father to them. That couldn't be more obvious right now considering how they've known you three days, and they're draped all over you in their time of need."

*What do I say to that?* I should say something because as horrible as Andrew has been, he looks completely and totally miserable right now. Hayes saves me from saying anything. He steps forward and hugs his father.

*Now, if only Emmy will agree.*

# Chapter Forty-Four

## Emmy

*We're going to be okay.*

Hayes and Audrey approach my bed cautiously. Can't say that I blame them. There's no telling what I look like. My head feels bloated to the size of a Macy's Thanksgiving Parade balloon. A vision of me floating down the street pops into my mind. I can't help but smile. *That would be the pain medication.* A quick thought of the pain in my shoulder, and the picture is gone. Despite all the drugs that must be coursing through my body right now, my shoulder is killing me. That's probably not a good sign of the days to come, but I will get through it. *I'm alive.* That's all that matters.

Well, maybe that's not *all* that matters. My children are with me. That matters, too. Audrey studies me with teary eyes. I reach out to her with my good hand, and she takes it in her own.

"Hi, sweetie."

My words come out weak. I clear my throat and try again.

"I'm going to be fine."

I wish that I could lean up and hug her, but my body now weighs about five thousand pounds, as if there's no way that I could possibly lift it from this bed.

"We were so worried, Mom."

*Hayes.*

My strong man. He stands behind his sister, a hand resting on her shoulder.

"Everything is going to be okay."

Even as I say the words, I'm unsure of their truth. We will move on, but their grandmother shot me. She tried to kill me. That isn't something that any of us are going to get over any time soon.

"You're right, Mom. Everything will be fine. Dad said that we can move to California with Jackson."

*Jackson.*

Just the sound of his name makes my heart squeeze.

"You spoke with your father?"

"Yeah, I'm here."

Andrew walks into the curtained area and stands at the foot of my bed.

"Kids? Would it be okay if I speak with your mother for a few moments alone?"

Hayes nods. Audrey leans over the bed and lightly kisses my cheek. They both leave without a word.

"I never knew that Hayes hides in your guest room when he comes over."

I'm not sure why that came out of my mouth. You'd think something like *your mother just tried to kill me* would have been more appropriate.

"Hayes hasn't been happy for a long time. I just didn't want to see it. Audrey isn't happy either, for that matter."

We stare at each other for many long seconds.

"I'm glad that you're okay, and I'm really sorry for what my mother did to you. Not just the shooting part." He winces. "All of it. That's another thing that I didn't see. She was so bothered that you had the Rutledge ring. She really wanted Carson to have it." He looks down at his feet. "I noticed that she seemed more chummy with you lately. I knew she was up to something, but I thought she would just eventually ask you for the ring back. I never thought her capable of this."

"Me, either. I knew she hated me, but I had no idea it was so much."

Andrew sighs a heavy sigh. "I'm sorry for lots of things. You, Hayes, and Audrey deserve more than I've given you. Wealth isn't a bad thing, but it isn't the most important thing. Love is. You have that with

Jackson. Hayes and Audrey love him, too. You should be with him."

"He's leaving for California."

"You should go with him, all of you. I will take care of updating the custody agreement. You all deserve to be happy, and it sure as hell isn't happening here."

Tears begin to fall. *I asked Jackson to leave. Am I too late?*

"I really am sorry, Emmy."

I nod my response. Speaking feels too difficult right now.

"Would you like to see him?"

"Who?"

"Jackson. They're only letting family back right now." *Well, you're not family.* "But, if you request to see him, then they will let him come back here."

*Jackson's here?* Suddenly it isn't so difficult to talk anymore.

"Yes, please."

***

*Jackson.*
*He's here.*

My ears strain to hear the words being said across the room. I hear only muffled voices—can't make out any of the words.

The curtain surrounding my bed moves, and then he's with me. The tears now overflow and slide down my cheeks. My eyes lock with his, those beautiful, blue eyes. He steps cautiously into my little cubicle and stands next to my bed in the spot previously occupied by Audrey. He's so close.

"I wasn't there for you when you needed me. I'm so sorry, Emmy."

"I'm the one who made you leave and then left town. If I'd listened to you, this never would have happened."

So many feelings mix inside me. What will Jackson say when he finds out that we can move with him? Will he still want us after the way I treated him? *But, he's here with me now.*

"It was Vanessa."

He places my hand between both of his.

"I know, sweetheart. I'm so sorry."

*Sweetheart.* Such a nice word.

"Where is she?"

"She's in surgery. One of the police officers shot her in the chest. They're not sure if she's going to make it, but I hope she does. She needs to pay for what she did to you."

*I'm not so sure about that.*

"Her family has money to pay for teams of lawyers. She might get away with it."

Jackson squeezes my hand lightly and begins caressing the back of my hand with his thumb. A small movement, yet it fills me with such peace.

"That's not going to happen in this case. There are plenty of witnesses. Smitty is in custody now.

Vanessa hired him to rob you that day. Smitty didn't want to do the dirty work himself, so he hired Castro and Martinez to do it for him. Smitty is the one who broke into your house the first time."

"Hayes was chasing a Navy SEAL?"

*Is it possible to feel even weaker?* Jackson leans over and places a light kiss on my forehead. The warmth of it spreads through me, strengthening each part of my body.

"There's also Marci. She's a witness, too. She saw Vanessa looking at locks at the hardware store. That's how they got in after I changed the locks. Many locks are keyed in pairs so that you can buy two locks for your home that use the same key. That just makes it simpler for people so they can use the same key for their front and back doors. Vanessa saw the code on the bottom of the package, bought another lock with the same code, and then used a key from that set to open your door when they went back in for the ring. Kind of ingenious, really."

"Vanessa told me that you were with Marci."

Jackson's expression becomes stern.

"I wasn't *with* Marci. She was waiting for me in the lobby of my hotel. Trust me, she was a very unwelcomed sight, but talking to Marci is how I learned about Vanessa being at the hardware store. That's how we knew to send the police to the beach house. If the policemen hadn't arrived when they did..."

"I'm so sorry that your friend let you down."

Jackson shrugs. "What Vanessa did to you is much worse. Why'd she do it? Did she tell you anything?"

Hopefully, in time I will be able to forget, but right now it's as if her words are burned into my memory.

"She never approved of me. Her recent niceness was all an act. She wanted the ring back, but once she had it, she decided that wasn't enough. She just wanted to be rid of me. I can't imagine what it feels like for Hayes and Audrey to hear that their grandmother is capable of murder. Grandmothers are supposed to be the safest women in your life. They're supposed to be warm and make chocolate chip cookies."

"My mom makes great chocolate chip cookies." He smiles.

*I guess this is it. It's now or never.*

"You were right, you know."

"What's that?"

He leans over me now, his face only inches from mine.

"What I told you was true. I don't want you to ever regret staying here with us, but there was more also. I was afraid of loving again. I was afraid of trusting someone again. I'm not afraid anymore. I love you, Jackson."

The corners of his mouth curl up into a smile.

"I know."

My own lips curve into a smile.

"I also know what Andrew told you tonight."

I feel my mouth open in surprise.

"Andrew told us outside in the waiting room. We can move anywhere in the world you want to go, Emmy. I just want us to be together. I love you."

*He loves me.*

Jackson closes the distance between us and touches his lips to mine in a feather of a kiss.

"You probably should know, though, that Hayes does want to move to San Diego. He wants to take up surfing."

"Surfing?"

Jackson shrugs. "I might have to try it myself. Do you like surfers?"

"I like you."

"That's all that matters to me."

"Are you sure, Jackson, that this is what you want?"

His eyes meet mine. They tell me everything I need to know.

## Epilogue

We left Williamsburg only one week later. There were some legal affairs to tie up and close out, but packing was unfortunately very easy. We went through the house and packed what we could, but other than clothes, almost everything we owned was broken or outright destroyed. It was sad in some ways but in others, perfectly okay. We bought new stuff when we got to California. It made for a fresher start.

Andrew came through with his promise to update the custody agreement. He says that Hayes and Audrey are welcome in his home anytime, but they are only mandated to go for two weeks each summer. That seems more than fair. Andrew also came through with the house. He's paying for the clean-up and any repairs needed to get the house ready for sale. That's only fair since his own mother is responsible, but it still seems like a feat since there isn't much with Andrew lately that has been fair.

Vanessa is still receiving treatment for her injuries. The shot went through one of her kidneys. There was some internal bleeding, but she's going to live. She'll be able to face justice for her crimes, and I'm glad.

My jewelry was recovered, even the ring. Vanessa had it in her bag at the beach house. Seems like an utterly stupid move, but it seems clearer and clearer that she wasn't of sound body and mind at the end. There's not enough there to go for an insanity plea—too much premeditation for that—but there's no denying the crazed look in her eyes when she pulled the gun on me.

The ring was sold to Andrew for one hundred and thirty seven thousand dollars. I had no idea that it was worth so much. That money is now in college funds for Hayes and Audrey.

Hayes and Audrey are doing great. They adjusted to new schools just fine. They are happy, and things are back to normal. They are back to fighting with each other instead of hugging constantly, but it's good to know that they have it in them when needed. They love our new house. We all do. Although Jackson and I have tried to take things slowly, it's been difficult to do so. We finally decided to throw caution out the window and just go for it. Jackson bought a house for us to live in. So, yes, I live in sin with my boyfriend. *Do they still call it that at thirty-seven?* Our house isn't as big as the house I left in Williamsburg, but that doesn't matter. This house is a home, and it's perfect. The kids have their own rooms, and Lucy has a fenced-in yard.

There are tons of kids in our neighborhood, and none them know about Hayes's and Audrey's looney grandmother. They only know about Jackson's mother, who's visited twice. She's asked Hayes and Audrey to call her *Grandma*, and they've complied. She has the same beautiful blue eyes that Jackson has and silver white hair that she wears in a bun. She's a little on the plump side. Yes, I'm painting a picture that seems a lot like Mrs. Claus, because she looks just like her. I've definitely grown to think of her that way. Maybe that's because she's baked cookies, made hot cocoa, and tucked the kids in at night with bedtime stories. I'm sure Hayes was just being polite at first, and I know he would deny it, but I think he likes it. These are just some of the things that Vanessa never did. Hayes and Audrey deserve this woman.

Jackson's father has been pretty excited, too. He took Hayes fishing on the pier last month when they visited, something Hayes had never done before.

Jackson and Marco have been working hard on their new business. Clients are lining up to work with them. It's great to see Jackson so happy when he comes home after a long day of working. He says that it's because he has us to come home to, but I know that it's more than that. He's happy being here in California and working with his best friend.

Jackson insisted that I stay home with Hayes and Audrey for the rest of the summer. Honestly, the time was wonderful. I was able to get us moved in, get acclimated to the area, and recover from my injuries. When the kids started school, I started looking for a job. Now I'm putting my new finance degree to use at a software programming firm. Life with Jackson is wonderful, and I'm the happiest I've ever been.

"What are you smiling about?"

I'm brought from my thoughts by Jackson's smiling face. We are at his parent's home in Phoenix. It's Thanksgiving Day and unlike any Thanksgiving my children have ever had. I always tried to make the day warm and loving, but we did always celebrate with Andrew's family. That meant a formal, dress-up, catered dinner. I didn't fuss because I wanted to make everyone else happy, but it wasn't ever very happy, and no one ever seemed very thankful.

This year is completely different. For starters, we're all wearing jeans. Hayes was thrilled to hear that he didn't have to pack a tie for this trip. We also made our dinner together, at least us ladies did. The men have spent most of the day on the couch in front of the television. Sure, they get out of the work in the kitchen, but it's okay today. Making Thanksgiving dinner is a group effort and usually plenty of fun.

During dinner, we all went around the table and

told what we are the most thankful for this year. I thought Jackson might cry when Hayes, Audrey, and I all said that we were most thankful for him. Jackson's mom did cry.

"I was just thinking about how much my life has changed since I met you."

Jackson sits down next to me on the porch swing.

"No more regrets?"

My lips curve up into a smile.

"No. None."

A huge smile spreads across his face. He stands, turns, and then kneels in front of me.

*Does this mean what I think it means?*

"I love you, Emmy. Hayes and Audrey, too. Marry me."

My arms move around his neck, and I hug him to me.

"I love you so much."

"Is that a yes?"

"Absolutely."

Dear Reader,

I hope you enjoyed *No More Regrets*. If so, please consider writing an online review. Reviews are very helpful and would be very much appreciated.

If you would like to be notified of upcoming releases, please sign up for my newsletter at www.tamralassiter.com. I'd also love to connect with you on Twitter or Facebook.

Sincerely,

Tamra Lassiter

# Acknowledgements

DISCLAIMER: Vanessa Bennett is completely and totally fictional and in no way reflects my own mother-in-laws. Yes, plural, as I have two. Many women can't claim to like their one mother-in-law. I've been blessed with two, and they're both fabulous. My father-in-law is as well. Much thanks to all the Lassiters for treating me like part of your family from day one.

Thank you also to my great friends and beta readers: Anne Newport, Trinh Goettlicher, Suzanne Bhattacharya, June Kuhne, Peggy Lassiter, and Pat Williams.

Special thanks to Mary McGahren for the incredible cover. You are truly amazing!

Thanks to Jena O'Connor of Practical Proofing, Toni Metcalf, and Mary Featherly for all your help with editing and proofing.